# FOURPLAY

### EVER AFTER DUET, BOOK 1

## JAYNE RYLON

HAPPY ENDINGS PUBLISHING

Version V4

eBook ISBN: 978-1-941785-93-5

Print ISBN: 978-1-941785-94-2

# ABOUT THE BOOK

It's normal to drool over three devastatingly handsome, charismatic, and rich AF men, right?

Well, not when they're your bosses.

Especially not if you find out they like to share their lovers and you can't stop fantasizing about being at the center of their attention during boring meetings.

And definitely not when you have a former co-worker who didn't understand the meaning of the word "no" harassing you.

But that's Kari's life, and now she needs to decide what to do about it: follow her heart, or forfeit the chance to discover what it's like to live out her wildest dreams.

*Fourplay is book one of the Ever After duet. Kari, Ford, Brady, and Josh's story will conclude in Fourkeeps*

# ADDITIONAL INFORMATION

# 1

Kari tried her best not to gasp or let her eyes bulge until they popped out of her skull and rolled across the polished boardroom table of the Westford, Arman, and King law firm, where she worked. Worse would be if she fell off of her chair. But seriously... What the fuck had Ford Westbrook just said?

She was pretty sure she'd heard her ultra-hot boss tell their intern, Cooper—who was in a polyamorous relationship with his girlfriend and her two other boyfriends—that, "We're really quite jealous of you. You see, the three of us have been looking for someone like your Andi. We just haven't found her yet."

But that would mean he and Josh King and Brady Armand liked to share the same woman in bed. Or maybe the woman would get each of them at different times. Three incredible boyfriends. Like any one of them on their own wasn't in the running for sexiest—and wealthiest—man in the city. Now Kari would never get the mental image of them triple-teaming some lucky lady out of her mind.

Or her wildest dreams.

Holy shitballs! That was going to make it hard for her to concentrate in meetings or during the time they spent alone together in her role as their executive assistant.

Kari understood then why the three big-shot lawyers had no intention of firing Cooper. Instead, they had turned on one of their employees, who'd ratted out a supposed ethics violation to the executive team. And that was even before they knew dirtbag Marty Schone had tried to blackmail Cooper into whoring out his girlfriend in exchange for Marty's silence.

It was too much to think about. Her brain was shorting out.

Despite her best attempts, a strangled squeak must have escaped Kari's suddenly very dry mouth because Brady whipped his stare to her. He studied her reaction to the bomb Ford had just dropped. The frown lines marring his handsome face made her wonder if he saw judgment rather than awe in her admittedly shocked gaze.

She flashed him a hint of a reassuring smile, hoping drool wasn't dripping off her canines. Surely they couldn't be self-conscious about their preferences, not if they had revealed them to their intern and to her in the process as well. But *damn*!

Kari subtly—she hoped—fanned herself with the manila folder she clutched in suddenly clammy fingers. It contained her own affidavit of alleged misconduct by good ol' Marty.

Right. The paper that said she'd been taken advantage of at a work function. The one that stopped just short of claiming she'd been raped, since she could never prove what she was finally coming to accept: Marty Schone had drugged her then abused her while she was inebriated.

There was no way she would have lifted her skirt for him anywhere, and especially not in the alley behind her place of employment while her three incredible bosses were steps away. She'd never found the guy attractive, and these days he sent chills down her spine if she so much as ran into him in the hall. Usually followed by a complete inability to eat whatever lunch she'd packed.

Maybe that was why Ford, Brady, and Josh had let her in on this part of their personal lives?

To make her feel more comfortable about what she'd been forced to admit to them...

What would her bosses think if all of a sudden she started acting like a cat in heat after the revelation of their lifestyle? They might retract some of the support they'd given her since her encounter with Marty had come to light. It had taken them a while to pry it out of her, but she couldn't hide the cold sweat she broke out in every time they were in a meeting with that scumbag. Once they'd realized what was freaking her out, they'd had her back. Completely and without hesitation.

Hell, she knew they were using Cooper's revelation to handle her situation, even if they didn't say it out loud.

Nothing meant more to her than that. They'd been there for her, even when she'd doubted herself. At first, her lack of memories from that night had made it difficult to understand what had happened. Easy to blame herself for drinking too much, given that she couldn't even say how many of those special holiday cocktails she'd knocked back.

Kari flipped open the folder and stared at the paper in front of her. The words "when I woke up, my panties were torn and dotted with dried blood and semen" blurred as her eyes turned glassy.

Josh King came over to her and squatted down by her side. His hand gripped the arm of the chair just next to her flesh, though he stopped short of making direct contact. Of course he did. He was her boss, not her best friend—though sometimes it felt like he might be both. The surprisingly deep conversations they had over lunch had become one of the highlights of her days.

For such a chill guy, he had a lot more going on underneath those smiles of his than most people would suspect. It was what won him cases. People tended to underestimate him.

She should be more like Josh.

Kari swallowed hard, resolve forming like a shield around her spine. The steely strength he lent her helped her sit straighter. If she had any chance at bringing Marty to justice for what he'd done to her and tried to do to Cooper, she would take it. And she couldn't be more grateful that her three bosses seemed to have exactly the same idea in mind.

Instead of flinging herself at them and crushing each of them in a bear hug like she wanted, she'd have to settle for a polite nod and an ultra-professional expression of appreciation. Because that's what their roles permitted. Now more than ever, she needed to remind herself of their workplace boundaries.

What they'd shared today hadn't been a secret confession from a man to his love interest. No, it had been the decent thing to do, done by three—four, if you counted Cooper, and she definitely did—very decent men she should stay far, far away from lest she do something wildly inappropriate. Again.

She scrunched her eyes closed, reminding herself for the millionth time since it had happened that she wasn't responsible for Marty's actions. Despite urging from her therapist, who'd gotten her to see that, it was still hard for her to fully accept.

Kari groaned inwardly as Cooper, Ford, Josh, and Brady wrapped up their meeting with huge smiles, back slaps, and the cementing of their growing personal and professional bonds. In fact, they'd just asked Cooper and his lovers to join the men on their yacht for Ford's floating thirtieth birthday party. Kari knew all about it because she'd gladly taken on making some of the arrangements. Helping to make it an incredibly special night had been like her own secret gift to him. She stood and shuffled toward the door.

"Well, we're hoping to see you all there." Brady beamed as he turned his head. It was as if he'd included Kari in the invitation instead of just the general conversation. She knew better than to assume that was the case. He was nothing if not polite and very practiced in social situations.

It took an enormous effort not to wince or flinch. She was pretty sure she'd seen the last of those gatherings. Would probably have a panic attack if she ever attended another function on her own anyway.

As if he could read her mind, Ford frowned in the background. "You'll be there too, right, Kari?"

"Me?" She shook her head as she stumbled back a step. "I don't think—"

"Maybe that would bring back bad memories for her. Don't push." Josh snapped to attention when he realized she was faltering.

"It's fine." She held her hands up, palms out, afraid they were getting the wrong impression despite her best efforts. The last thing she wanted was to cause tension between the three partners and best friends. Not after they'd done so much for her.

"Guys, calm down." Brady stepped between them, his voice calm and soothing as always. It settled the flutters in Kari's stomach and gave her time to sneak in a deep, if shaky breath.

Kari murmured, "Thank you."

Ford scrubbed his hands over the dark stubble hugging his strong jawline, then nodded. "I just want you to know that it's my birthday and I'd love to have you there, if you're up for it. No pressure. The whole office won't be coming, either. Not like the last party. This is a personal gathering, not a company-wide one. If you join us, we'll make sure you're protected. Okay?"

Did he really think she was worried about that? No, she was more concerned she'd have too much to drink and hit on him or one—or both—of his partners. This time maybe she'd be the one to cross the lines and screw things up.

It had always seemed like a messy situation, flirting with one of them while fantasizing about what it might be like to go on an actual date sometime instead of a working lunch. Now that she knew they might like to share, she wouldn't have to pick which of them was her favorite. Hypothetically speaking, she could have all three. At once.

*Oh God.* "I just don't think—"

"No pressure," he repeated.

They let it drop. Maybe because they were glad she didn't plan to take them up on it. Or maybe because they really did respect her hesitance. After they walked out of the boardroom, they acted like it had never come up.

Kari should have been relieved. Except that damn party was all she could think about for the next several weeks. Every time she took a call from the caterer about the gourmet food they'd be serving or decided on flower arrangements or set up designated parking with the marina or hired a local up-and-coming DJ to provide entertainment for the night, she felt like Cinderella dreaming of the royal ball.

Where was her fairy godmother, damn it?

## 2

---

"It's probably best if you don't stare at Kari's ass considering she's already been traumatized by a dumb fuck she works with." Brady knocked his shoulder into Ford's.

Josh noticed even the physical jarring didn't dislodge his friend's gaze. He tracked the woman until she rounded the corner to her office.

Josh couldn't quite blame him. Sure, every instinct he had was screaming to chase her down and make sure she was okay. The lawyer half of his brain admitted that wasn't all, though. He wanted to comfort her, smother her in hugs and gentle kisses until the ragged emotions he'd seen in her eyes during their meeting faded away. Then he'd confess that he'd been dreaming of being more than her friend or boss for months.

But if Brady took issue with them staring at her, he certainly wasn't going to approve of that sort of intimate advance. More importantly, Kari wouldn't welcome it either. That was the only reason Josh didn't pursue her.

"No. She was traumatized by a dumb fuck she *worked*

with." Ford spread his feet and crossed his arms, making his suit jacket rumple. Josh felt like it was in danger of bursting at the seams. Sort of like him and his two best friends. "With Cooper's statement about Marty's blackmail attempts, we've got him by the balls. He's gone. I can't wait to drag his ass in here and break the news."

Josh tipped his head to each side, cracking his neck in the process. "Let me call the security guard for the building and make sure he's ready to escort that douchebag out of here after we've had our little chat. I don't think we should take any chances. He might go ballistic on Kari or Cooper when we wipe that smarmy tattletale smirk off his fucking face. For that matter he might come for us. As much as I'd love to introduce my fist to his face, none of us can touch him, not even in self-defense."

"Because you don't trust us not to seriously fuck him up?" Brady asked with a growl that made Josh pretty sure he would be right in that assumption.

"Right. But also because we don't want to leave ourselves even a tiny bit exposed to a malicious lawsuit from him. We need an impartial witness and someone official to do any manhandling required." Ford's mouth twisted into a snarl. They all knew how badly he wished he could kick Marty's ass on the way out the door.

"Then let's do this." Josh gestured toward the landline conference phone on the boardroom table. "The sooner he's gone, the better off we'll all be. Kari especially."

"Guys, even once he's out, it's not going to change things. Not enough. Kari still has to live with the issues Marty's attack caused. We've got to be careful around her," Ford droned on, lecturing them like always. Josh tamped down his irritation. The man was doing what he thought was best, trying to protect a woman they all cared strongly for. "Besides, we're lucky she hasn't sued us for giving him the opportunity to attack her. I wouldn't even fight a suit if she brought one against us. We should have done a better job looking out for her...and the rest of our employees, of course."

Josh snorted. Each of them knew Kari was more than hired help to them. Hell, she kept their lives in order. Without her, they'd never be able to operate the business —or their personal lives—half as efficiently as they did with her overseeing operations. During the five years she'd worked for them, she'd become an integral part of their team, blending into the executive unit seamlessly.

"Zip that up, Ford. Your guilty conscience is showing. It kills me as much as it does you to know what happened right under our noses." Josh put a hand on his friend's shoulder. "But that doesn't mean we're responsible for someone else's actions."

"Hmm." It wasn't an agreement. Not even close.

Ford had always had a savior complex, ever since his own mother had been abused by her boyfriend and he hadn't been able to stop it. Each of them volunteered at the animal shelter just to keep him from filling their penthouse with a herd of misfit pets they weren't home often enough to care for properly.

Brady backed Josh up. "He's right about that."

"Fine. Then all we can do now is support her and help her recover. Not make things worse." Josh wondered if Ford was talking to them or reminding himself at this point. "Besides, she's closer to Cooper's age than ours. How stereotypically pervy is it to lust after your young, gorgeous administrative assistant? Even if she was by some miracle into the freak show we're after—"

"No. You're not going to do that anymore." Brady swiveled to face Ford. "Beat yourself up for how you're wired. Go ahead. But you're not going to make me or Josh feel like shit for our desires anymore."

"Looks like our intern taught you a thing or two today." Josh tried to cut the tension with a quick jab and a quicker grin.

It was more than just a joke, though. Cooper had marched into their office and proudly proclaimed that he and his roommates were in love with the same woman. That they shared her between them without drama, respected her and each other. He told them he was proud of the affection they showered her with. Dared them to find fault with it or call it immoral. Even if it meant losing his job—one they knew he'd busted his ass for—he didn't give a single fuck.

And neither should they.

Maybe one day they'd evolve that far, but for now—and during the ten years since they'd met in college—they had other priorities. There was too much at stake to gamble their firm on people's reactions to their unconventional tastes in bed.

"Can we at least agree that the most important thing here is Kari? Making sure she stops jumping every time someone comes up behind her in the copy room and that those damn rings under her eyes start to fade?" Ford asked while glaring at both Brady and Josh.

"Of course." Brady nodded, the frown he'd been wearing lately in danger of becoming a permanent fixture on his face.

"Yeah." Josh didn't debate that. Maybe Ford was right.

Even if Kari had once been the right person for them, Marty had stolen their chance to prove it to her.

And for that, in addition to all the rest, he hated the fucker.

"Good. Then I think it's time we had a chat with Marty Schone." Ford cracked his knuckles.

"Better keep those jammed in your pockets. Just in case your legendary control slips for even a moment." Brady raised a brow.

Josh shook his head. He'd have to rein in his own temper if Ford was that close to the edge. Otherwise their rage could feed off each other's as their emotions sometimes did. They couldn't afford to do this wrong.

Asshole or not, Marty was still a shark of a lawyer. They wouldn't have kept him on at the firm this long if he hadn't had a stellar record in the courtroom. If they left him any opening at all, he'd use it to come back and bite them in the ass.

"I'll keep my shit together," Ford promised. "But we're going to need to hit the gym hard tonight. Maybe do some sparring."

"I like my face too much for that. Maybe we should swing by a club instead," Josh suggested. It could be the only way to work Kari out of his mind. He'd wanted so badly to lift her onto his lap and rock her earlier when her pain had bubbled up to the surface.

Except he didn't have the right to touch her, and never would.

They needed to find someone else. Even if it was a poor substitute for the woman they each had been eying for months. They had to channel this energy arcing between them before someone got fried.

"We'll see." Ford didn't sound convinced. Guaranteed he'd have some excuse to avoid going. Lately he seemed to be losing interest in the casual liaisons they'd had with women. The ones that had kept them all sane and sated despite the pressures of their career and the desires they couldn't quite seem to satisfy.

Something had to give.

Josh just hoped it wasn't Marty Schone's deceptively pretty face.

Ford picked up the phone in the middle of the conference table and hit zero. "Hi, this is Ford Westbrook. Could you please send up the security officer we discussed earlier? Thank you."

They paced the elaborate meeting room, ignoring the gorgeous view out the expansive windows until their chaperone arrived a few minutes later.

There was only one thing left to do.

Together, Ford, Brady, and Josh took out the trash.

# 3

TWO WEEKS LATER

"I know Ford already told you there's no pressure, but...you *are* coming tonight, aren't you?" Josh's neon green stare pierced Kari, making her squirm in her seat. It was thrilling to be asked, even if she didn't plan to take him up on his invitation.

As if he could sense her answer, he continued trying to convince her. For a lawyer skilled in cross-examination, it was probably as close to no-pressure as he operated. "I mean, you took care of so many of the details, it's virtually your own party. It wouldn't be right if you didn't enjoy the fruits of your labor. Especially that killer black raspberry cake you commissioned. I've been dreaming of it ever since that tasting you took us to at lunch last month. You know Ford so well. The anchor design was perfect for him, and he would love it even more if you were there to enjoy it with us."

Over the top of the giant monitor on her desk, Brady glared at Josh. Was it because he disagreed?

She did her best to ignore Josh and focus on his partner instead. "Don't worry, I won't be crashing tonight.

I totally understand that you don't feel comfortable with putting me on the guest list after what happened at the Christmas party…"

"What?" Brady snapped his stare to her and it was ten times as intense as Josh's had been. "Do you really think I would hold that against you? Kari, I'm pissed because we agreed not to harass you about coming. Ford is going to be furious when I tell him Josh is bugging you about it."

*Oh, that. Right.*

She nodded softly. It would always be there, hanging between them. Embarrassing her and freaking her out at the same time. Making her second-guess herself and causing them to tiptoe around her. A tiny part of her appreciated it, even though she mostly hated the need for special treatment.

Kari would be lying to them all—herself included—if she denied the anxiety wringing her guts at the thought of attending another party any time soon.

Hell, she'd ended up in the corner of her sister's bathroom, hugging her knees and shuddering, just last weekend. All because her nephew had invited some poor kid named Marty to his pool party. She'd taken one look at the clown-shaped goodie bag with that name written in bold Magic Marker across the top and nearly passed out.

Then she'd spent the next half hour trying to keep her sprinkle-laden birthday cupcake down while telling herself over and over that she was safe, until her reflexive self-defense mode came off of red alert. When her fingers had stopped shaking, she'd doled out a couple of the anti-anxiety pills she'd resisted taking, and surrendered.

At least there, she'd been a quick Uber ride from home. No one needed her to lose it while they were out at sea. They'd have to turn the entire yacht around to get her back to shore once they passed out of range of the dinghy. No way was she going to make a scene like that in front of Ford, Brady, and Josh. Not ever again.

"I appreciate the gesture, Josh. Honestly, I do. I just don't know if I'm up for it yet." *Or ever.*

He extended his hand toward her, but Brady lunged across her desk and swatted it away before he could make contact that he hadn't specifically asked permission for.

She knew Josh meant well, but still, she loved that Brady was looking out for her in his own way, too. With these guys—and Ford—around, she felt sheltered in the best of ways. Protected. That was more valuable to her than the fat paycheck she took home. It made her crave their presence. It also made that tiny sliver of her old self that Marty hadn't squashed debate the foolishness of staying behind instead of joining them tonight, where they could both take care of her and give her the chance to have some fun again.

In a purely platonic way, of course.

Kari mentally rolled her eyes. Even she didn't believe the bullshit she was trying to sell herself.

Was she justifying her desire to hang out with them outside of work? Probably. Until right then she hadn't been aware that she was waffling, considering showing up at the last moment. Her hesitation as she questioned her own sanity stretched the silence between them until it became extra awkward.

Josh's shoulders slumped. "That was insensitive of me. I'm sorry. I understand if you don't—"

"Hey, it's fine. It's nice to know you still want me to come. Especially after I caused so much trouble last time." Kari's cheeks heated as she thought back to the police reports they'd filed, the investigators poking around the office, and the showdown with Marty. That was before she recalled their endless patience with her when she spaced out or fucked up during the months she'd spent coming to terms with what had happened and how it might not have been a bout of temporary insanity on her part, but something far more sinister.

The day she'd broken down and admitted to both herself and them that she suspected she'd been the victim of a date-rape drug had been one of the most mortifying and simultaneously cleansing of her life. Ford had immediately called the police and asked them to take an addendum to her statement. Brady had offered to drive her to her counselor's office, and Josh had acted like absolutely nothing was wrong or different with her, cheering her up by continuing their ongoing cat meme war via texts when she teetered on the verge of darkness.

Brady disagreed. "*You* didn't cause anything." The steel in his tone left no wiggle room.

"At least we agree on that." Josh crossed his arms as if fighting the urge to extend them toward her again. "Nothing that happened the last time was your fault. I hate that it's still causing you pain and suffering now. I guess this was my way of trying to make up for it. And set things right, you know?"

"It's not about you. It's about her," Brady snapped.

Some of Josh's reasoning got to her, though. She supposed that's why he was so good at his job. He was persuasive, logical, and capable of building undeniable arguments.

"Hang on." She put her hand up and both of them shifted their gazes to her. The intensity of being caught between them made her a little dizzy and a lot reckless.

"Maybe I'm crazy, but what you're saying makes some

kind of sense." She took a deep breath, then looked at Josh. "It could be good for me..."

"So we'll see you at the dock tonight?" he asked with a widening grin. "Or, if you prefer, I could send our limo to pick you up at your place."

Of course, that reminded her that even her best dress wasn't really suitable for a soiree of this level. It had been foolish to dream of it. Because now she was twice as disappointed as before that it wasn't going to happen.

She winced, then admitted, "That sounds incredible, but I'm really not prepared. I don't have anything to wear, for starters."

"There's still more than seven hours until you need to be ready. Take the afternoon off. Go shopping. Do girly shit." Josh waved toward the door. "Do what you've got to do and we'll send the car for you at six."

Her mouth might have slipped open. Was he serious?

"You know, that's not a terrible idea." Brady looked at his gorgeous, sophisticated watch. The one Josh and Ford had custom designed to commemorate his thirtieth birthday. It reminded her of what a big night this was and how desperately she wished she could share it with them. "There's plenty of time. You worked at least that much overtime last week while we were prepping for the DePaul trial."

That was true. In fact, she'd easily put in twice that many hours but hadn't marked them all down in the time-keeping program the firm used. "Are you sure?"

"Yes," both men said in perfect unison.

Then Josh continued, "Use the company credit card as our thanks for all you do for us. We really appreciate how far above and beyond you go. I'm sorry I didn't say so sooner."

They had told her often enough. Kari couldn't even bother to correct him when she was still reeling from his generous offer. She waved her hands in front of her, hoping they didn't think she was trying to take advantage of the situation. "That's not necessary."

"We know, but we would like it if you took us up on it. Buy yourself a pair of really expensive shoes and a new purse while you're at it. Seriously." Brady shrugged. "What's the point of having money if we can't use it to make people we care about happy? Besides, Josh procrastinated and didn't end up getting Ford anything for his birthday. It'll go a long way toward making up for it if you come and he gets the credit."

"Hey! I framed that old goals checklist we made back in college now that we've hit them all, but yeah...it's pretty lame." Josh stuffed his hands in his pockets.

"No, it sounds sentimental. I'm sure he's going to love it." Her heart melted a little. These guys were people she wanted to spend more time with, and if they were going to lavish some of their generosity on her, maybe she should accept it.

"Not as much as he'd appreciate your company," Josh insisted.

Kari swallowed then, trying to clear the lump in her throat. He seemed completely unaware that his kindness had punched right through the thick wall she'd built after Marty had taken advantage of her. To know that they cared, that they still valued her contributions to the firm and—just maybe—beyond that as well... It meant a lot.

There was no way in hell she was going to disappoint them or herself.

She was going to do this. Wipe away every bad memory and replace them with good ones.

"Okay." She opened her desk drawer and drew out her wristlet. She zipped her phone into it, then shut down her computer.

"Seriously?" Josh lit up. He grinned then squeezed her in the briefest of hugs before Brady yanked him back again.

Kari smiled, her mouth remembering what it had been like when she'd done that a hell of a lot more often. Maybe she could again soon, too. "Yep. I'll see you guys later. And...thank you. For everything."

"Remember, go wild," Josh said as she walked out the door.

Kari raised her hand, waving with a chuckle. It seemed that instead of a fairy godmother, she had a pair of fairy godfathers.

Hell yes, she did. Bippity-boppity-booyah!

# 4

Kari hadn't quite realized what it would be like to ride in the back of the guys' private car all by herself. It sounded fancy as fuck, having Bronson—their driver, a pretty cool retired military guy who sometimes chatted with her at the office when he was waiting to whisk them off to court, meetings, or home after a long day—pick her up right at the curb of her building and take her to the docks. No cursing at traffic, no long-ass walk in impractical shoes, no sweaty commute on packed public transportation.

Actually, though, it was kind of creepy. Like she was being kidnapped. That thought did nothing to still her tapping toe or her fingertips drumming on her knee. So she half-stood and leaned forward until she could rap on the dark divider between her and the driver's seat.

It rolled down, letting in the late afternoon glow and a view of the sherbet-colored sky.

"You okay, Ms. Hill?"

She snorted at that. "It's always been Kari. Still is, you know?"

"You've never been the guest of honor at one of my bosses' shindigs before."

A nervous laugh squeaked through her tight throat. "I'm not tonight either. I'm a pity invite from the office."

He glanced at her in the rearview mirror, one eyebrow raised. "You don't really believe that, do you?"

She shrugged her shoulder, feeling air brush over the bare skin there. Nothing like the times she'd ridden with the guys on the way to a professional event while fully buttoned up in one of her many boring, colorless suits. Would they like the dress they'd bought her and all its sparkly flair?

"If you do, you're nuts. Those boys adore you. When I left them, Brady and Josh were even more excited than when I bring them pizza. Josh was bragging about how he got Ford the best birthday gift of all time and how he planned to take all the credit. Brady didn't seem to care much since it meant he was going to spend time with you."

"Seriously?" Kari sat a little straighter at that insight.

"Of course." Bronson cleared his throat. "And when they see you...looking like that..."

His soft whistle of appreciation was exactly the confidence boost she needed to keep from begging him to turn the car around. Kari settled back into the seat.

The silence extended between them as they each turned to their own thoughts. It startled her when he cleared his throat. "I shouldn't really be telling you all that, but it's weird, because I know you and... Well, I've never seen you nervous before. You rule that office like it's your own personal army. Need me to turn the air up some more?"

"Please." Maybe then she wouldn't feel like she was

about to pass out. Kari wiped her damp palms on her thighs. "Tonight is different somehow."

"Just my personal opinion here, tell me to shut up if you want—"

"No, go ahead. I can take it." She braced herself for him to tell her she wasn't ready to be Cinderella at the ball and should go back to filing court documents and making appointments instead.

He paused, then said, "I've seen this coming for a while. Don't know why it took so long. Probably because of that asshole who used to work at the firm. Farty Marty. Always stinking up this car after hammering the garlic bread at that shitty Italian restaurant he loved for lunch meetings."

While mention of the M-word usually had her poised on the verge of a heart attack, Bronson took the scary right out of her attacker with that nickname. There wouldn't be any hiding it if he let it rip in the backseat while Bronson was driving him to or from court or one of the other times the guys had generously lent the driver's services, which Marty had never failed to request.

Kari put her hand over her mouth and cracked up.

"Anyway, something changed. A couple of weeks ago." Bronson kept his stare glued to the road, but she knew he was using his observation skills to pay close attention to her reaction. "You don't have to tell me what it was or anything, but they're different. On edge. Short with each other. And...hungry."

Kari knew exactly what it had been: Cooper. His courage to stand up for the life he wanted had inspired the partners and inadvertently rubbed their noses in something they craved but didn't have.

Ford, Brady, and Josh always got what they wanted.

What if that was her?

Crazy thinking. Absurd. That's what that was. They'd asked her to come tonight because they'd been through some shit together and it had made them grow closer. From colleagues into something dangerously like friends.

They wanted to make things right, and so did she. Have an epic do-over to ease their consciences and help her heal, get past her fears. That's it.

Before she could set Bronson straight, they turned into the marina. He rolled up as close as possible to the dock, then parked and got out. They had arrived.

Bronson opened her door and extended his unflinching hand to her. He blocked her view of the docks with his broad back. She figured he was shielding her from at least one of his bosses' stares when he looked down at her kindly. "You ready? I can drive you back home if you prefer."

A gulp of air later, Kari put her fingers in his and let him assist her so she didn't flash anyone in the process of getting out of the car. He kept a hold on her until she was steady on her feet despite the wicked heels she'd picked to match her dress.

While she oriented herself, he coached her quietly.

"You look great. They're going to be so glad you actually came." He squeezed briefly, then released her. "Remember, you have my number. Call if you need me to come get you. Anytime. Whether I'm working for them or not, I'll be there to take you home. You know, in case something doesn't go as planned..."

Rumors spread faster than a wildfire in their office. Plus, the guys spoke openly around Bronson. Did he know everything that had happened to her or was he guessing at the source of her stress? Either way, she appreciated his support. "Thank you."

He nodded, then stepped aside.

Sure enough, Josh and Brady were just beyond him. Brady leaned against the railing, his hands planted on either side of his hips as if clinging to the wood to keep himself tethered there. Josh had no such reservations. His smile transformed into a full-fledged grin as he approached her like a puppy welcoming its owner home after a long day of work.

"Kari! You look...incredible." He clasped her in a brief but enveloping hug before releasing her so he could take in her entire outfit.

"We'll see if you still think so when you get the bill. Thanks, by the way. I had a hell of a time this afternoon." It had been downright decadent to have someone at the upscale boutique pamper her. First in selecting the perfect dress and then handing her off to a stylist in their sister salon next door to ensure her make-up, hair, and wax jobs were up to par with the gorgeous outfit.

"Worth every penny." He didn't flinch. "And your hair. Damn, I didn't realize how long it is."

Because she'd never worn it like this at the office. Winding it into an immaculate bun was part of her morning routine. Loose, it flowed in soft curls over her shoulders and most of the way down her back.

"You look great yourself." That was an understatement. He could singlehandedly cause a spike in the designer's sales if the tabloids got a shot of him rocking that tuxedo. From the look of it, Brady's matched. If Ford was sporting the same one, the three of them were going to melt the panties off every woman on board tonight.

Hers were no exception.

She tugged the hem of her dress lower on her thighs. A beaded, sheer crimson overlay lent the illusion of modesty to a daring, shape-hugging satin sheath beneath it. Or at least that's what the saleswoman had tried to convince her.

Of course, her adjustment only revealed a bit more of her cleavage than she'd intended. *Shit*! Kari mentally kicked herself for failing to consider the transfer out to the yacht and how much of her legs it would expose to be climbing in and out of a dinghy. The gangplank dotted with antique glass lanterns and the flowers she'd arranged for would make it as easy as possible. Gorgeous as well, if she did say so herself.

Josh held out his arm to her, and somehow her hand wound itself around it. It felt right for him to steady her as he brought her toward Brady. Every step closer made her more aware of the smoldering stare Brady leveled in her direction.

His eyes barely twitched, but she knew he'd scanned her, beginning at the tips of her ridiculous heels, stopping only when their gazes collided. The intensity of his admiration hit her square in the chest. Heat blossomed within her. He didn't have to say anything.

His wide almond eyes communicated his appreciation loud and clear. "Josh is right. I'm never going to be able to top this."

Josh laughed and Brady shook his head ruefully before saying, "You're absolutely stunning tonight."

She began to thank him, except just then the crew started ushering guests into the dinghy. Kari tried to stick to the balls of her feet. Still, her heel managed to catch a crack in the planks and make her wobble a bit.

Both men, one walking on either side of her, reached out simultaneously.

She took their hands in hers, glad for the excuse. Touching them, even this harmless little bit, gave her the courage to climb aboard when part of her began to cringe at the thought of what lay ahead.

"You sure you want to do this?" Brady murmured as Josh glared at him. "It's not too late to change your mind."

Kari nodded. "I'm good. Let's go."

At Brady's nod, the crew set off in the direction of their yacht, which waited for them, anchored out in the harbor. The seventy-foot catamaran took up a lot of space in their local marina and the guys preferred to leave her on the hook to discourage uninvited stowaways from sneaking onboard. Kari couldn't say she minded that policy after what had happened last time.

Even from a distance, it was easy to spot Ford, standing tall on the port side of the boat, waiting for the first load of guests to arrive at his party. He looked perfectly at home on the vessel, as if he were the captain of some highly profitable historic merchant marine ship with a hint of pirate dashed in as well.

As they neared, she realized his arms were crossed and his feet spread to keep him steady on the gently swaying boat. That did absolutely nothing to diminish the impact of his incredibly sexy—and yes, matching—tuxedo. The booming voice he used when presenting an argument to the court now greeted his guests instead.

The dinghy pulled up to the back of the yacht and steadied near the sugar scoops, where steps led up to the entertaining areas. When Ford's stare landed on her, tucked between Josh and Brady, his smile faltered for the briefest of seconds.

"I'll go if he doesn't want me here," she whispered to Brady. "I can take the tender back when they pick up the next load of passengers."

Brady held her hand tighter. "Don't leave. I mean, unless you want to. Trust me. He's not going to send you away."

Josh laughed as Ford's grin returned, with interest. His eyes sparkled in the twilight. "How in the hell did you manage this? What a lovely surprise."

He brushed aside the crewman and held his hand out to Kari directly. Brady put his palm low on her back and helped her stand, while Josh lifted her fingers to Ford's. They worked seamlessly together, ushering her toward their partner.

"Welcome aboard, Kari."

"Happy birthday," she murmured close to his ear as he helped her across the gap and onto his yacht with an arm around her waist. It might have been the waves, or maybe her instincts, but her lips grazed his cheek as his strong arms settled her onto the deck.

"It certainly is now." He held her close as she proved she'd paid attention to their guest instructions and removed her heels. It was a polite gesture on his part, she was sure, as crew members did something similar, if less personal, for the rest of the guests.

"You can thank me later," Josh teased Ford. He laughed as he collected her shoes, then said, "I'll put these inside for you, okay?"

Kari nodded. The last thing on her mind then was the shore or any possibility of leaving this party early. Hopefully, the night would last forever.

## 5

----

Did Ford have to smell so damn fine? Like the sea, and whiskey, and...pure man?

Kari would have been the world's worst liar if she said it didn't do incredible things to witness admiration and maybe even a bit of heat in his gaze. He murmured, "Thank you for coming. I promise, tonight will be a hell of a lot better than last time. Anything you want or need. Anything at all, just let me know."

The prickling in her eyes and the lump in her throat made her nod then scurry off for some air. She didn't want him to see her sad and weak. She wanted to be the strong, elegant woman she'd dressed as for the night. Even if that meant she needed a moment to get her shit together first.

Before Kari could second-guess her decision, Brady was yelling *anchor up* from his place near the gypsy while Josh trimmed the sails and Ford steered them out of the harbor. Although they had crew to do those things for them, she knew that sailing was one of their simple pleasures. It was the reason they'd opted for a catamaran rather than some sleek powerboat. Relying on nature, the wind, and their combined skills helped them cope with the stress of their demanding careers. Watching the three of them work together to launch the boat into the night warmed her from the inside out.

There was a reason they were so successful. They were an amazing team. One she liked to pretend she was a part of from time to time while she assisted them.

Kari hoped she wasn't deluding herself about her place among them because that gave her comfort, allowing her to believe she fit in enough to attend this not-so-professional party. The twinkling lights of the city began to shift as the shore fell farther away. There was no escaping it now. She was on board until they returned. So she might as well make the best of the evening.

A male chuckle rumbled from behind her, startling her. When she glanced over her shoulder, she saw a young woman stumbling toward the railing, looking a little green. Three guys trailed her.

"It's not fucking funny," the woman hissed at her companions, her auburn hair swirling around her, making her look fierce if adorable. "I don't want to puke on your bosses' boat."

Kari could relate. Being humiliated at a fancy event like this... Well, at least she'd come prepared for the easy stuff. She turned to the woman, who now gripped the steel cable lifeline not too far away, and said quietly, "I have Dramamine. Would you like some?"

"Oh!" The woman blinked Kari into focus then nodded her head, a wince following closely on the heels of the motion. "Yes, please. Thank you. I think I love you."

Kari grinned even before she realized who it was that came out of the shadows to accept the medicine on behalf of the woman.

"*Everyone* loves Kari," Cooper, the firm's intern, said with a gigantic smile. They'd bonded that day in the boardroom, when the depths of Marty's betrayals had come to light. Both of them had suffered at his hands, been made to think there was something wrong with them and their sexuality because of that bastard. Ever since then, they'd shared a special friendship. One she was grateful for and would love to expand. Curiosity about the woman who'd snagged not only Cooper, but his two hot friends, threatened to make Kari ask a million questions before she'd even said hello.

"Hang on...*you're* Kari?" Andi paused, her arms unwrapping from where they'd been hugging her stomach before she flung them wide and smothered Kari in a warm embrace. She was a world-class hugger, Kari admitted to herself. At first awkward, she returned the gesture, the vial of pills still clasped in her fist. "I'm so sorry. I hope it's okay that Cooper told me. You know, about what happened. That guy is a monster. *So* creepy. I hated him from the first second I saw him."

"You met Marty?" Kari knew for sure Cooper hadn't brought Andi to any work functions before. He hadn't worked there when she'd been attacked, and Ford, Brady, and Josh hadn't had another get-together since. Well, not until tonight. And this was a totally different sort of thing.

"Oh. Yes. That's how he figured out that we were all together. He saw me once with Cooper then later with Simon, and assumed I was cheating on them." Andi's nose wrinkled. "I might be a greedy bitch for wanting my three guys, but I'm damn well not some backstabbing liar."

Kari grinned, then shook a couple pills into Andi's palm. Cooper handed her a glass of water to wash them down, which she did before draining the rest of the drink.

A gorgeous antique ring glinted on her left ring finger. It was an obvious symbol of their commitment.

Huh. How would that work exactly? Kari didn't know, but she really wanted to find out. Tonight could be even more enlightening than she had imagined.

"Hey, I'm Reed. Would you like me to get you one of those or maybe something stronger?" asked a tall, dark-haired man—one of Cooper's other roommates.

"No!" Kari realized she'd practically shouted when Andi, Cooper, Reed, and Simon each leaned back, their eyes wide. "Thank you. I mean, no thank you."

A flood of memories threatened to drown her. *Picking up her drink from the bar at the Christmas party. Laughing as she sipped it, setting it down only briefly while she ran to her office to grab something Marty had requested. Him handing it back when she returned. Her with a dizzying headache, stepping out into the alley for some fresh air. Marty coming to check on her. Him crowding her against the rough brick wall. A blur of what had happened after...*

It didn't matter that the bastard wasn't there now and that she was among friends. She wasn't about to impair herself in any way. Not tonight and maybe not ever.

Kari blinked back tears. Maybe she hadn't been ready for this.

"Would you mind coming and sitting over here with me?" Andi asked Kari softly, shooing her guys away. "I still feel kind of queasy and I'd really appreciate your company."

Kari knew what the other woman was doing, offering her support while appearing to need it herself, but she didn't give a flying fuck right then. She latched on to the arm Andi held out. Together, they wobbled across the enormous rope net trampolines at the front of the catamaran and plopped down cross-legged, side by side, riding the gentle waves.

For a while, she listened to the splash of the water and let the power of the full white sail above her head scrub the lingering memories from her mind. Eventually, she faced Andi. "Sorry about that. It sometimes sneaks up on me."

"I know it seems like just something people say, but it really does get better with time. And with people to talk to who understand what you're going through. I could give you the name of my therapist if you want." Andi smiled, but the corners of her lips were twisted.

"You too?" Kari hated that for a moment she was happy. Pleased to have someone who could relate to the terror, disgust, and hopelessness that raged inside her when she least expected it. "Wait. Not Marty?"

"No." Andi shook her head. "It was about a year ago. A stranger at a club. He drugged my drink and assaulted me. I was lucky the guys interrupted him before things went...too far."

Kari was quick to correct Andi. "I don't believe that. Sounds like it went plenty far. Anything at all is too damn much if you didn't agree to it."

"You're right." Andi sighed. "See, even now it's easy to get caught up in the lies we tell ourselves after trauma like that. But it does get better. I can go out dancing now, if Cooper, Reed or Simon are there, too. And...well...being intimate with them, it's not a problem."

Kari stifled a groan. "I've been worrying about that. I haven't...not since..."

"You just need the right person, or *persons*." Andi winked. "Don't look now, but there are a certain three super-hot lawyers who are ignoring my fiancés and staring at you instead. They're concerned about you. And, it seems to me, not only as their employee."

"It's not like that between us." Kari shook her head.

"I bet it could be if you wanted it to be." Andi laughed then. If it meant letting her play matchmaker for a moment to distract her from her seasickness, Kari figured she could take one for the team, even if it was wild speculation. "Sorry. Don't mean to push. I'm just saying they seem pretty great to me and Cooper told me that they're poly, like us. I guess I just want everyone else to be as happy as I am these days. It seems like you could use a little of what they have to share. There's nothing like having three gorgeous, powerful men worshipping you to empower a girl."

Well, since Andi had brought it up... "How does that work exactly? Do you take turns or what?"

Andi grinned, reminding her of a lioness licking her lips after devouring a gazelle or three. "Sometimes. More often lately, it's a group affair. I'm spoiled, I know. I forgive you if you want to hate me for it."

A laugh burst from Kari. She tipped her head back and reveled in the cool breeze blowing her hair. It felt like it was taking all her problems with it. Good thing too, because the scene she was envisioning—one with her in place of Andi and her bosses instead of Cooper and his roommates—was hot enough to spike her temperature.

"Oh yeah, I know that look." Andi knocked her shoulder into Kari's as they whispered conspiratorially. "You have it bad for them."

"I won't say I haven't thought about it since that day, when they told Cooper what they're searching for." Kari fanned herself. "I guess it's even more appealing because I trust them completely. Lately, that's a characteristic I find highly attractive and hard to come by. But they're so far out of my league it's not funny."

"Shut your face, girl." Andi smacked Kari's knee. "You're absolutely stunning, smart, and a good friend to one of my guys. Cooper tells me how you rule that office and keep a bunch of absentminded, arrogant lawyers on their toes. In fact, he brags about you so much I told him I was going to try to steal you away for the firm. We've been recruiting for a position in my department and every person we hire just makes more work for us. It sounds like you would be a perfect fit."

"Thanks, really. But..." She looked over her shoulder, busting Ford, Brady, and Josh staring at her and Andi. Were they worried about what Andi might tell her? Or did they just want to make sure she was okay?

"Yeah, I get it. I wouldn't want to leave them either." Andi crossed her arms and pouted. "I figured, but I had to try. If you change your mind, I'm sure we could make it worth your while."

Kari doubted that. The guys paid her extremely well, and she did her best to earn her generous salary. But tonight wasn't about work. It was about having fun. "You feeling better now? Up to rejoining the crowd?"

Andi nodded. "Much. Thanks for the medicine, and the distraction. I hope you're steadier now, too."

"I am, thanks." And she meant it. Her nerves had evaporated. Knowing Andi was there, and that she could relate, went a long way toward making Kari calmer. "If I end up locking myself in the bathroom tonight, will you talk me off the ledge?"

"Absolutely. If you start to panic, come find me or have one of the guys do it." Andi put her hand on Kari's and squeezed. "You've got this. And even if you don't, there are plenty of people here who will be glad to pick you up and help you try again, okay?"

Kari got to her feet, then extended a hand to help Andi to hers. Briefly, she hugged the young woman, and smiled. "How about we sample some of the food? I picked it out and I promise you it's going to be fucking delicious."

They were still talking and laughing when they piled their plates high and joined the guys in the cockpit. The look Ford shot her was one that surpassed hunger. She might have thought he was starving, except he waved her off when she offered to share.

Andi shot her a glance that clearly said, *See! What did I tell you?*

Subtly, Kari shrugged one shoulder. She focused on the exquisite flavors bursting over her tongue instead of the gazes she felt trained on her. Not only Ford, Brady, and Josh's, but also Cooper, Reed, and Simon's. Plus those of all the other curious guests who milled about as the eight of them spent most of the evening together in conversation.

They had so much in common, aside even from work. She found it fascinating to hear the guys talk about sailing, the boat, and antics from the years they'd known each other.

She was surprised when the last of the dessert trays were removed and the music grew louder. Had so much time passed already? Whereas earlier she'd feared making it through the entire event, now she wished she could slow the evening to make it last for a year or more.

"Doing okay?" Brady murmured. He leaned in closer to hear her response over the music and conversations. It was a hell of a party. One people would be talking about for months. And not because of some poor office girl who'd been raped this time either.

"Amazing." She beamed up at him. They had no idea the gift they'd given her tonight. It was one she would always treasure. For the first time in months, she felt like herself again. Better than herself, because she knew how strong she could be if she needed to be. And how they would do the heavy lifting for her when she couldn't do it herself.

"Do you want to dance?" Josh asked.

"Hey! It's my birthday. I think I get the first dance." Ford cut in front of Josh and held out his hand. It was strong, unwavering, and so damn inviting.

Kari glanced over at Andi, who flashed her a not-so-subtle thumbs up. What was the code here?

Rather than stress out about rules she didn't know how to play by, Kari did what felt right. She laughed, then put her fingers in Ford's but also grabbed Josh's sleeve. "Nothing says we can't dance together, does it?"

"Only if I get to come, too." Brady edged up behind her. Rather than feeling trapped between the three men, she felt...at home. Shielded and free to let loose.

"I insist," Kari said with a smile, then let them whisk her onto the trampolines, where people congregated and some, at the core of the crowd, were making the most of the festivities. She was about to be one of them.

## 6

Kari sang along to song after song as she
danced, sometimes at the center of the three
men and sometimes pairing off with one, or
being sandwiched between the other two of them. They
felt amazing in every combination. It unleashed
something within her that hadn't been loose in a very long
time. Maybe ever.

She felt it deep within her when they changed course
—both shifted, the direction of the boat and her
perception of the three men with whom she was enjoying
spending time.

Part of her mourned the dying night and feared the
loss of everything that had happened out here at sea.
When they went back, would they return to being bosses
and employee?

She wished their personal trajectory could be altered
as easily as the route of a sailboat. Never before had she
wished to veer sharply off the straight and narrow path
she'd followed her entire life.

"I'm going to help the crew navigate to the anchorage."

Ford brushed some of the hair that had escaped his usually neat style back into place. She preferred it wild. It would look even sexier and more rumpled if he'd fucked her instead of merely dancing with her.

Where the hell had that thought come from? Kari put her hand on her chest to keep her heart from leaping from her ribcage when it skipped a beat.

"Will you be okay by yourself if we go help?" Brady asked her.

"Of course." She smiled. "I think I need a breather anyway."

It would be nearly impossible to fill her lungs with enough air after her vivid mental image of Ford in bed. Maybe she could find Andi for another discussion. It felt like her whole world had changed in a matter of hours. What was she getting herself into?

Worse, maybe it was nothing to them and she was setting herself up for disappointment and an awkward-as-fuck work environment.

Lost in thought, Kari wandered to the life lines that ringed the edges of the boat. Unlike earlier in the night, she didn't cling to them. Instead, she stood tall and faced into the wind, letting it cool her off. She must have stood there longer than she realized, because when she opened her eyes, she was alone on that part of the boat. Most of the passengers were congregating near the cockpit as the shore grew closer.

One of them had been introduced to her by Josh earlier as Dr. Ansh Patel, a renowned neurosurgeon, the youngest to ever sit on the board of directors at his hospital. A man used to this lifestyle and seeing her bosses with far different women. He stared at her now with enough curiosity that she realized people were wondering about her and how she fit in with Ford, Brady, and Josh. As was she.

Kari peered into the distance but didn't see Andi, her guys, or Ford, Brady and Josh for that matter.

Making small talk with strangers didn't appeal, so she settled in to wait her turn on the dinghy back to shore. She relaxed, content to let the flutter of her extravagant dress mesmerize her, light flashing off the beaded sheath. The one her bosses had bought her.

*Bosses.*

Not friends.

And certainly not anything more than that.

It would be best if she remembered the distinction.

With a sigh, she pried her eyelids open in time to see most of the other guests had already been ferried ashore by the tender while she daydreamed. It was funny. That gorgeous wooden boat would be most people's primary vessel, not merely a dinghy for a monstrous catamaran.

It figured Ford, Brady, and Josh had the best. Going small wasn't their style. They had offices on the top of the tallest building in the city, an exclusive clientele list that grew by the day, and the highest billing fee to go along with it. Hell, they probably had big—

And that was it. She had to get out of there before she veered into dangerous territory or thought about how they could also have the most amazing women, ones far more refined and desirable than her.

Kari pivoted and headed for the crew member helping the final few guests cross the gap between the catamaran and the tender as they rocked in slightly different patterns. Right before she joined them, she remembered the shoes Josh had taken from her and stowed in the galley earlier. While she'd enjoyed strolling around the fiberglass, rope, and polished teak barefoot for the evening, the gravel parking lot would be an entirely different matter.

"Oh." She glanced over her shoulder toward the interior cabin.

"Forget something?" the crew member asked.

"My shoes." She nodded.

"Would you like me to get them for you?" He winced as he raked his gaze over the passengers in the tender.

"No, stay here with them and I'll be right back. Or I could grab the next one if that's easier." She smiled softly, oddly thrilled when he latched on to her suggestion.

"If you don't mind, I'd rather do that than bob around for a few minutes. I don't want anyone getting sick. Especially since most of them have been drinking."

Right. She wouldn't want that either. "Go ahead. I'll be ready when you get back."

Kari waved him off when he double and triple checked, then headed for the interior of the boat to hunt down her heels.

"Damn it." She wasn't trying for any awkward goodnights or goodbyes. Slinking away unnoticed—like her Cinderella idol—would have been much preferable than causing a scene.

Especially if they were taking some time to show Cooper, his girlfriend, and her other two boyfriends around the yacht since they'd all seemed to have vanished. Though Kari longed for a tour herself, she had declined their earlier offer. Going below decks in tight quarters with Ford, Brady, and Josh might lead to her plastered up against one of them due to the gentle rocking of the boat. Not to mention her building desire to touch them.

44

How was it possible that they looked even better in the tuxedos they'd worn tonight than the killer tailored suits they wore to court?

Kari fanned herself as she peeked inside the main cabin, hoping to find her shoes sitting right at the entryway. No such luck.

The galley and salon were buried in refreshments and supplies for the caterers, the DJ, and the florist. No room for guests' belongings there. So she crept to one of the two stairways leading into the hulls and the private living space within them.

It looked like someone had been using it as a shoe rack. There was a pair or two on every tread, including hers, near the bottom. Yes! Kari climbed down and crouched to grab the gorgeous stilettos.

That's when she heard it.

A moan. Of pain, or something else?

The soft sound drew her forward, her curiosity impossible to resist. Kari crept along the remaining stairs, then peeked around the corner into the captain's quarters.

Andi sat on the edge of the bed—massive by any standards, never mind nautical ones. Her eyes were closed as she leaned against Cooper's chest. He held her in his arms, so carefully and yet securely enough that she wouldn't slip despite the motion of the boat and the sensations that had to be coursing through her. Because one of her boyfriends was kissing her while the other massaged her feet.

What might have started out innocently enough seemed to be escalating as his hands wandered along the bare skin of her legs, which was exposed by her gorgeous red dress.

Cooper cleared his throat, then said, "Well, we'd better head home before things get out of hand."

"Hey, don't stop because of us," she heard Ford rumble. What was he doing there? "Tonight, don't think of us as your employers, please. Here, we're not."

Did that count for Kari, too? If so, maybe she would be bold enough to announce her presence and join them. What would happen then?

"I'd like to see what it could be like, if we were as lucky as you." Brady said quietly. The raw emotion in his voice tugged at Kari, urging her to take a step closer, though she didn't dare.

Kari should have fled. She should have plugged her ears and ran back to the tender waiting to ferry her to shore. Put an entire ocean of cool, dark water between herself and temptation.

She didn't. Part of her lectured herself, *this is probably how you got yourself in trouble last time*. And the rest of her tried to stomp out those insidious voices. The ones that emerged at night and blamed herself for Marty's actions.

Hell, it was Andi who had told Kari not to listen to those terrible things she thought about herself.

And maybe she could see why. See what it was like to be part of a healthy relationship. She wanted to discover what it was like when a woman was the center of all that very wanted, very focused attention.

Just for a moment, she promised. Then she would go. Before she invaded their privacy too badly. She clung to the wall of the stairwell to steady herself, though it had more to do with her insides rioting than the subtle sway of the boat in the bay.

Cooper looked to his friends and then to Andi, who nodded. He smiled as he slid his hand inside the top of

46

her sweetheart neckline to cup her breast. Ford shifted in his seat, cupping his obvious erection. Kari's eyes widened. Both because she was more turned on than she'd ever been in her life, and also because she realized she was intruding on a more personal moment than she'd intended to spy on.

It wasn't right for her to do this. To look when they hadn't given her explicit permission. Having been violated herself in that way, she'd never be okay with watching without their consent.

Kari backpedaled, jerking around so fast that she slipped.

She stubbed her toe on the step and had to fling her hands out in front of her to keep from taking another one to the face. "Shit!"

"Hello?" Josh called. He'd been sitting closest to her hiding spot.

*Oh god no!*

# 7

---

**K**ari tried to concoct some plausible reason for why she'd wandered down to their private space, but she couldn't think that fast when lust and mortification hazed her brain. So instead, she took the coward's way out and ran.

"Hey, who's there?" Josh said, louder—and distinctly less friendly—this time. His question was followed by footsteps. She wasn't going to make it before he spotted her. "Kari? Is that you?"

She froze. No point in fleeing now.

"*Kari*?" Ford echoed.

"Son of a bitch!" Brady added.

Hushed murmurs followed the revelation. Everything down below went silent.

"Yes, sorry, Josh. I came to find my shoes." She held up the heels and wiggled them lamely in the air. "Got 'em. Going home now. Didn't mean to interrupt."

Josh looked over his shoulder then, probably at Ford and Brady. He said, "I've got this. You guys stay. It's fine. I'll handle it."

Kari couldn't say she liked the idea of being a problem to *handle*. She figured it wasn't the first time they'd had to think of her that way either. Damn it. Things were already reverting to how they'd been before this precious time-out had made her believe she was making progress.

She began to walk backward, slinking out of the boat's cabin, wishing she could melt through the floor and drip into the ocean. Dissolve and disappear. "I'm sorry. Truly. I shouldn't have looked. I didn't see much. And I won't say anything. I swear."

Josh didn't relent. He pursued her, taking a step forward for every one she took in reverse. "Are you sure, Kari? You didn't see anything at all?"

Her shallow, rapid breathing, wide eyes, and rock-hard nipples probably gave her away.

She had to get outside. Needed fresh air to breathe properly.

Kari wasn't proud of herself, but she pivoted on her heel and bolted.

Behind her, Josh cursed beneath his breath. He followed. "Kari, wait! It's fine. I'm not mad. None of us are."

She was running out of room. Even their boat wasn't big enough for her to hide from him when he was in direct pursuit. She bounded across the trampolines at the front of the boat until she could cling to the life lines once more. For a wild second, she debated the likelihood of making it to shore if she dove in and swam.

The stars reflected in the inky black waves beneath her blurred as tears flooded her eyes. She'd screwed things up. Again.

This time it might cost Kari her job in addition to her pride.

Josh came up behind her, slowing as he approached. The ropes creaked softly as he crossed them, inching toward her. "Hey, it's okay. I'm sorry if I startled you."

"I'm going to take the next boat ashore. I'll be out of your hair in a minute. I won't move from this spot until then, I swear. I understand if you don't want me to come back to work Monday either." She sniffled. What the hell was wrong with her?

After having her own privacy so brutally invaded, she should have respected theirs instead of peeping on them.

"Kari, look at me. Please," Josh begged.

It took everything in her to turn around. When she did, she squeezed her eyes shut rather than see disappointment or hurt on his handsome face.

"I swear, it's fine," Josh whispered this time. From somewhere closer. Then closer still when he said, "I really want to hug you right now. Would that be okay?"

"What?" Her eyes flew open. He was standing right there in front of her. Easily within arm's reach.

"Just a hug, Kari. I think we both could use one." He held his arms open to her.

Without a second thought, she flew into them and buried her face against his chest. "I'm so sorry."

"Please stop saying that," he murmured into her hair. The sweet gesture made her realize that he was off balance, too. She wrapped her arms around his solid body, clinging to him or helping him to stand tall himself, she wasn't sure which. "It's good that you were interested. I'm happy that what Marty did to you hasn't stopped you from being curious or wanting to experience intimacy with someone. I hope we didn't frighten you or bring back bad memories. That's the last thing we would want to do."

Kari shivered in his hold.

She pulled away just enough that she could look up into his deep blue eyes, the color the ocean had been before that spectacular sunset earlier. His blond hair was rumpled, reminding her of how he'd been lounging, stretched out on the divan of the captain's quarters just a minute ago, and the hours they'd spent dancing, nearly as close as they were now.

She much preferred those natural, open Joshes than the uncertain, guarded one she could see emerging. So she decided to be honest. "I haven't really been interested in anyone since then. But what I saw down below...that was...*wow*."

Josh smiled then, slowly and softly. "Seriously. It was intense even though they were hardly getting started. Amazing, right?"

She nodded, biting her lip to keep from begging him to take her back inside so they could watch whatever was surely unfolding below, guilt-free this time.

No, that was too much to ask for. More than she could handle after what had already been a monumental night of breakthroughs. She couldn't risk fucking that up now.

Still, she didn't want to take anything away from Andi, Cooper, Reed, and Simon or her bosses, who'd been soaking up their honest passion. "It was. She's lucky. Andi, I mean."

"No, I think the guys are the fortunate ones." Josh sighed then. He rubbed her back in soothing strokes up and down her spine that seemed natural for him. She'd bet he didn't even realize he was doing it as he composed his thoughts. "Have you ever wanted something so bad, but didn't believe you'd ever get it? Or that it was even possible? I'm not sure if it makes it better or worse to be that close and see what we don't have. No amount of hard work or money will guarantee it happens, either. It's a situation the three of us aren't used to being in."

"You're frustrated." She leaned into his touch then, hoping to give him some comfort in return.

"More like scared," he admitted. "What if we never find our Andi?"

Was he crazy? What woman wouldn't want to be pampered and adored by three of the sexiest, funniest, most noble men she'd ever met?

"You will, Josh. You will," she promised him, wishing she could have been the one for them. If only things hadn't gotten so complicated, maybe... "You guys are some of the best men I've ever met. Any woman would be lucky to have you."

He paused then and went stiff beneath her fingers. His muscles coiled as he looked down at her, peering intently into her eyes. "*Any* woman? Including you?"

Kari blinked. How should she respond? Honestly? Or in the way that was best for their professional relationship?

At the end of the day, she couldn't bear to see him struggle with his emotions or the self-doubts she'd fought for so long now. "Yes. Especially me."

His hands shifted, moving upward. They left her only briefly, so that he could bring them in front of her and cup her face in his palms. He tilted her head back and lowered his own until his lips were a hairsbreadth from hers.

"Tell me now if this isn't what you want," he whispered.

Kari couldn't speak the words necessary to get him to stop. She didn't want him to. Instead she went up on to her tiptoes and sealed their mouths together. He groaned and applied himself to their kiss. Their first kiss, and maybe their only.

If it was the one chance she ever got with him, she wanted to make it count.

Kari twined her fingers with his short blond hair and held him close so that she could absorb the world-rocking impact his caresses had on her body, and her life. Nothing would be the same after this. And she didn't care. It was so good. She had to have more.

She parted her lips, snaking her tongue out to lick at him, to taste him more fully.

He followed her lead and deepened the kiss, pulling her tight to him as he sucked on her tongue, making her knees wobble.

When she might have fallen, he lifted her. Thankful for the stretch in the oversized, gossamer outer layer of her dress, she wrapped her legs around his waist to steady herself. It might have been unladylike, but there was nothing civil about what she was sharing with Josh as they made out.

She moaned into his mouth and began to squirm slightly, rubbing herself along his entire torso. The hours he spent at the gym were very apparent in his tight ass beneath her calves, his flat abs—which pressed against her core—and the rippling muscles in the shoulders she clung to. Despite his hardness, which she could now unmistakably detect pressed between her legs as well, she felt something else coming from him.

Tenderness, affection, awe. Things that were far more dangerous.

Things that frightened her.

So she broke their upper bodies apart. Her hands kneaded his pecs as she tried to catch her breath. Their foreheads rested against one another and they stared directly into each other's eyes.

"Kari?" he murmured.

She didn't know how to respond. Didn't know what he wanted or where they were supposed to go from here.

Her hesitation affected him, too. Some of the passion darkening his eyes began to fade and that damned uncertainty crept back in. "I'm—"

"If you say you're sorry right now, I swear I'm going to knee you in the nuts," she blurted before she could think better of it.

Fortunately, it seemed to be exactly the right thing to say.

Josh cracked up. He squeezed her tight, then lowered her to the trampoline as her legs loosened their hold on him. "So noted."

Kari grinned up at him, his amusement infectious.

Besides, it was such a relief. Maybe she hadn't spoiled everything by ogling the group down below or by kissing him. How that could be, she wasn't sure, but she figured she should stop while she was ahead. In the distance, the tender approached. Her carriage had arrived.

The entire evening had left her reeling. Swamped by so many different emotions and revelations. She truly felt like Cinderella must have at that ball. But now it was long past midnight, and she had to return to reality before she turned into a pumpkin.

"I think that's my ride," she said softly as she lifted her chin toward the approaching boat.

"Ah, okay." Josh nodded solemnly. "Feel free to say no…"

Was he about to ask her to stay? Tell her he wanted her to rejoin them downstairs, as an approved guest this time? She hoped not. It wasn't an offer she could accept. She had to salvage this night and her job. Her pride.

Besides, they both knew it wasn't up to him. Andi, Cooper, Reed, and Simon weren't here to give their permission. No one was going to interrupt them now.

"Would it be okay if I took you myself? Back to shore and then to your house? I would feel better making sure you get there safely." He ran his fingers through her hair, straightening it as he waited for her response. It was a little unfair, because his gentle caresses sent sparkles through her bloodstream, making her agree, even if she shouldn't.

"I'd like that." She stepped back, but trailed her hand down his arm until she could link their fingers together. She'd allow herself that simple, innocent touch to keep herself steady.

Even if it was reckless.

Because part of her could imagine what it would be like if she was really his. His and Ford's and Brady's. And she liked that vision too much.

Josh lifted her fingers to his mouth and kissed her knuckles, every bit the chivalrous prince she imagined him to be. He guided her toward the sugar scoop, where they met the tender.

After a brief exchange, he took over for the crew, officially releasing them from duty for the evening. Neither she nor Josh said much as they returned to shore, and real life, especially not with other people around. That didn't mean she couldn't feel his stare on her or the pulses of heat in her lips as she replayed their kiss over and over.

Kari touched her mouth, wondering if she would always feel the press of his there. It was far better than the last encounter she'd relived a million unwanted times.

She looked up at Josh and smiled, then mouthed, *Thanks*.

*Anytime*, he mouthed back.

When they reached the dock, he hopped out first then handed her up next before swooping her into his arms. Shocked, she clung to his shoulders.

"Since we never went back for your shoes and this is gravel..." He kicked a few rocks then trailed off when she didn't argue.

Kari didn't want to admit it, but she felt so much better with Josh carrying her through the shadows of the harbor parking lot then tucking her into the limo, that she didn't even mind Bronson's speculative gaze. She only regretted having to let go of him.

This time he kept the divider firmly in place, though he didn't need to. She and Josh were on their best behavior as they shared a quiet ride back to her apartment. He kept hold of her hand, but didn't make any other advances.

When they entered her neighborhood, he murmured, "Are you okay?"

Surprisingly, she wasn't lying when she said, "Very. I'd say tonight was one hell of a success."

"Me too." He squeezed her fingers, then brushed his thumb over her knuckles, making her shiver. Before anything else could happen, they'd arrived. He climbed out and reached for her. She didn't even bother to protest when he gathered her against his chest once more.

He was a perfect gentleman as he brought her inside, rode up the elevator, set her down on the carpet outside her apartment, and waited for her to unlock her door. It took a few tries since her hands trembled with the desire to turn and cling to him again. She hesitated on the threshold, but didn't ask him to come in. There was too much to think about for that.

Josh nodded, as if he agreed with her unspoken decision. He leaned in briefly, only to dust a friendly peck over her cheek. "Goodnight, Kari."

"It was. One of the best," she said.

"I agree, and only the beginning," she thought she heard him murmur as he turned to go. Kari was sure her building had never had a man as fine as him inside it, and it was a shame to let him leave.

But when he slipped into the elevator, she sighed, and locked the door behind him.

To keep people out, sure. But also to keep herself from running to catch him.

What the hell were they going to do now?

## 8

J osh sat in the main living space of their penthouse, surrounded by glass and steel. He hadn't bothered turning the lights on, preferring instead to crash on the white leather sectional and survey the cityscape, gleaming even in the darkest hours of the night. From here, he could barely make out the marina in the distance. He rolled the tumbler of whisky around in his hand, ice cubes inside clinking against the sides, before taking another deep drink. He let the amber liquid pool on his tongue then swallowed, relishing the burn of the aged liquor that meant soon he'd be numb.

Although, frankly, he'd thought that several glasses ago. Nothing was alleviating the ache in his chest that had blossomed when he'd torn his lips away from Kari's and worsened when he'd turned his back on her at her door. She wasn't his to claim. And she never would be.

*Damn it.*

He remembered shouting her name as he sprinted after the whirl of silk and long wavy hair she'd turned into as she fled. Had she been running from him or from what she'd seen?

Or from the fact that she'd liked it?

He'd noticed the awe and envy on her face when she saw how Cooper, Reed, and Simon worshipped Andi. Hell, he'd recognized it because he felt the exact same way.

Plus horny.

*Really* horny.

Of course, his hard-on had wilted the moment he'd realized what had happened—that she'd stumbled across a situation she might not be ready to process and which could easily have triggered bad memories. Then he was bounding over winches and lines to reach her before she vanished in the tender. Getting laid had been the last thing on his mind.

Okay, maybe not quite the last, but her safety and mental well-being had been way higher on his list of priorities. So he still wasn't sure how they'd gone from him comforting her to him kissing her. Nothing in his life had felt more right and yet probably been as wrong.

The whole point of inviting her to Ford's party had been to help her forget and heal. Instead, he'd complicated things by turning the last moments of the evening into something delicious but treacherous. He'd be lucky if she didn't slap him with some sort of sexual harassment violation.

Putting enough distance between them to see her home had been painful. Leaving her at her door instead of bringing her to their penthouse or asking if she'd wanted to stop somewhere for late-night dessert or if he could tuck her into bed and watch over her while she slept... Well, keeping silent had just about resulted in him having to bite his tongue off. It had taken every shred of willpower he possessed to keep the questions from flying from his lips, which still flamed from their kiss.

There had to be a better solution. One that worked for each of them.

It wasn't often that Josh wanted something he couldn't have. And he didn't fucking like it.

Not at all.

He'd been sitting there stewing for who knew how many hours before he heard deep, familiar laughter and the excited voices of his two partners echoing down the hall from the front door, which opened off the private elevator that serviced the building's penthouse. They'd been friends for over a decade. It had seemed natural to get a place together while they were in law school. As they'd advanced their careers together and upgraded their home, they hadn't seen any reason to branch out on their own. Their lives meshed through both business and friendship.

Everyone said that was a bad idea, but Josh had never been afraid of the repercussions of melding their lives so completely...until tonight. Kari could change everything. For the better if they were lucky, or much, much worse in the bulk of the scenarios he could conjure.

That didn't stop him from wishing for the improbable or ruminating over every possible way he could make it happen for them. Brooding was more Ford's style, or maybe even Brady's. He'd be happy to give them back this burden, if only it were that easy.

Brady burst into the main living space first. He ambled to the couch opposite Josh, his tux jacket draped over one forearm. Undone, his bowtie hung on either side of his shirt, which had been unbuttoned some. He tossed his jacket across the back of the sofa, then took off his polished shoes, kicking them to the side of a plush rug that helped define the wide open area that made up their living room, dining room, and kitchen.

Never before had the enormous space felt so cavernous and empty to Josh. It sure as hell did now.

Walls would be a shame in a place that had a view like this. Open inside, only the perimeter delineated the space. Even that was entirely made of glass to ensure each direction held amazing sights of their city. But Brady wasn't looking at it tonight. And neither was Ford, who followed behind more slowly. He shrugged out of his own perfect jacket, which didn't have a single wrinkle despite him wearing it all night. He hung it neatly on a stool at the bar nearby before untying and arranging his own shoes.

Only then did he join his friends, his gaze trained on Josh. He frowned when he took in the glass Josh clutched.

"You okay?" Ford sobered pretty quickly, his satisfied smirk melting off his face.

Josh's self-loathing kicked up a notch. It wasn't often Ford relaxed and enjoyed himself. His birthday party had been a rare treat, and now Josh was about to fuck it up. Maybe he should just keep his mouth shut and go to bed. They could fight in the morning.

"Fine." He left it at that.

"Ah, shit." Brady scrubbed one hand through his midnight hair. "That's bull."

"Sorry you missed out on the fun. I thought spending time with Kari would help make up for it." Ford grimaced. "But you're right. It's not fair you had to leave just when things got good."

"Huh?" Josh tilted his head. Maybe he'd drunk more than he thought. His friends weren't making any sense.

They thought *he* was pissed at *them*? That he'd gotten the short straw that night?

"Not to rub salt in the wound or anything, but for the sake of full disclosure..." Brady couldn't help but revert to lawyer mode when he tried to solve problems. It was how they were programmed. "Cooper and his family put on one hell of a show for us. After watching how they worshipped Andi and brought her so much pleasure... fuck, I've never wanted something more."

His hand wandered to his crotch and he rearranged himself. It didn't do much to disguise his arousal.

"It was incredible," Ford agreed. "Hot as hell. I don't think I've ever been so fucking jealous of an intern before."

He looked around the spectacular place they lived, as if assessing its worth with fresh eyes. Josh did, too. Whereas in the past he'd thought it was perfect, he realized it wasn't quite a home yet. Not without someone to bind them together and fulfill their fantasies. To fill the massive void threatening to swallow him whole.

Things would be different if Kari lounged beside him on the rich white leather or brightened the place with her gleaming smile or the sound of her humming to herself while she was working. It was easy to picture them making breakfast together then getting in a food fight that resulted in the three men devouring her instead.

"Damn," he groaned.

"Seriously." Brady nodded. "Do you want details or not?"

Josh blinked. The guys were still unaware they were having two totally different conversations. Fuck it. He might as well let them distract him from his transgressions and from the longing that threatened to drown him. "Yeah, sure. What happened after I left?"

*Besides the most intoxicating kiss of my life, that is.*

As if a dam had burst, Brady said in a rush, "Once they realized we weren't about to object, I think Andi really got into showing off for us. Like she finally got to flaunt her guys to someone who gets it. She was passionate, so generous and affectionate with them. It was like she knew what each of them needed and made sure they had it without even trying."

"What he means is that Andi has a lot of needs of her own and each of them fulfills some of them. She gets off on it when Reed takes control, but Cooper and Simon reassure her and soften his harsh commands." Ford threw his head back, letting his skull rest on the back of the couch while the tendons in his neck stood out. He gazed upward, then slammed his eyes shut.

Josh knew that was one of his major concerns when it came to a life partner. Ford had some sharp edges himself. It reassured him when his best friends were present during rough encounters to make sure he never went too far in the heat of the moment. Josh was man enough to admit that Ford took liaisons places he wouldn't have been comfortable on his own, but enjoyed being along for the ride.

It might have been weird to some people. Over time, it had become natural for them. It was just that they'd always thought their ménages were a wild indulgence of their younger days, not something that could blossom into a mature and lasting relationship.

Not until they met Cooper and his family.

Having hope was almost harder than before they'd made that discovery. It made him crave what Ford was describing that much more. They were ready to make this transition in their life. But was Kari?

Unlikely.

At least he could live vicariously through his friends for a little bit. "So how far did things go?"

"All the way," Ford responded without hesitation.

"They fucked in front of you?" Josh nearly dropped his drink.

"Don't add a bunch of romantic comedies to my Netflix queue or anything but...no, I wouldn't say that." Brady cleared his throat. "They made love together and I feel fortunate to have seen it for myself."

"I can't even call you a pussy." Ford grabbed Josh's glass and downed the rest of the whiskey before admitting, "I felt the same way. They touched her like she was priceless. Even Reed when he was hammering into her. His hands were caressing her sides and he kept murmuring shit into her ear that I couldn't quite hear. It was so different than what we've been doing."

"So much better." Brady scrubbed his hand over his face.

"It went deeper than getting off." Ford leaned forward, planting his elbows on his knees as his stare bored into Josh. He'd never seen his friend this intense, this convincing, outside of a trial. "Although when they did... Son of a bitch, I thought they might blow a hole in the side of the boat and sink us all right there. It was explosive."

"I get it, guys. It was the most profound sexual experience of your lives and I missed it." Josh sighed. He wasn't really irritated with them. Besides, he'd had one hell of a consolation prize. It was just that kissing Kari had been incredible but ultimately undermined by walking around guilty with a hard-on ever since, and here the two of them were trying to rile him up even more.

But why didn't they seem equally as frustrated as he was?

"Hold up...did you guys do more than watch?" he asked, squinting as he stared at Brady's hands. Sure enough, his friend curled his fingers and began to tap them on the outsides of his knuckles.

Josh pointed at his tell and half-shouted as he bolted to his feet, "You bastards, you did!"

"They didn't seem to mind how much we appreciated their display. In fact..." Brady looked at Ford, who nodded. "I didn't really think about it, but I started to rub my dick. Andi noticed right away. Instead of freaking her out, it seemed to turn her on. Next thing I knew we were—"

He paused to clear his throat, and Ford finished for him. "We jacked off while we watched them have sex. It was wicked and intense and...damn. It's *everything* I want for us."

Josh felt the weight of his cell phone in his pocket.

He could text Kari. Would she answer? Would she tell him to stay the fuck away—him and his two perverted best friends?

He'd never put her in a position to have to do that. Not after how she'd already been taken advantage of by a manager in their own company. No way.

But son of a bitch, he wanted to. The device was practically burning a hole in his pants.

Or maybe that was his cock. It was rock-hard and begging for relief.

Okay, this had been a bad idea. Instead of distracting him, Ford and Brady were making him hornier and he had no outlet for his pent-up desire. "I think I better go to bed."

"Go to watch porn on your laptop in your suite, you mean?" One corner of Ford's grin kicked up. "Yeah. Me too. Let's go."

Brady beat them to the stairs, as eager as them for some alone time. Except Josh wished it wasn't so…lonely. His shoulders slumped as he climbed the winding staircase. Bright white marble steps with no back were held in between glass half-walls and crowned by a chrome railing. It curved up the long stretch between the first and second floors of their penthouse to their private quarters.

At the top, the cool stone gave way to plush carpet. His suite was to the left, Brady's to the right, and Ford's generally in front of them. It was past a door they didn't talk about often and none of them ever opened.

They paused on the landing there, each of them doing their best to ignore that extra space now and failing miserably.

"So, anyway…" Ford slapped Josh on the shoulder, then squeezed it in his version of a hug. "Thank you for making tonight the greatest birthday of my life. For getting Kari to come in the first place and then taking care of her while we played voyeur. You really are the best friend a guy could ask for."

"I'm not even going to argue." Brady shrugged. "You outdid yourself tonight, Josh."

"You're a shitty lawyer," Josh muttered as he turned his back, feeling like the exact opposite of the champion they'd made him out to be. Truth was, he was afraid to admit it and let them down.

So he didn't.

Brady and Ford cracked up, as if he'd been joking. Josh

didn't know whether to be relieved or terrified. Because when they found out he was a sham, the revelation would have the power to break their friendship.

"I'll send you links to any good group sex videos I find. Then you'll forgive me," Brady promised.

If only he was the one who had pardoning to do, Josh wouldn't be so upset. If he lost his best friends on top of everything else, he wasn't sure what he would do.

## 9

The next afternoon, Kari was sitting on her couch, binge watching some dumb show about blind dating. While it had entertained her in the past, the idea that some random guy out there was the one for her no longer appealed.

She'd spent the entire day trying not to think of Josh, their kiss, or his two partners.

What a fucking mess.

More than once, she'd grabbed her phone and thought about using the firm's emergency contact system to call Cooper at home and beg to talk to Andi. She'd hadn't had the guts.

It shocked the shit out of her when her cell shattered the silence and started buzzing like crazy.

Unknown number.

Screw that. She wasn't in the mood to listen to scammers or spammers. Kari sent the call to voicemail. As soon as she did, it rang again. Same number.

Prepared to rip a telemarketer for bugging her, she

was surprised when a familiar voice shouted, "Hey, it's me! Don't hang up. Please!"

"Andi?" Kari sat up straight.

"Yeah. I got your number from Cooper. I hope that won't get him in trouble or anything." The woman sounded genuinely worried.

"Of course not. I actually was thinking about doing the same." Kari twisted her hair around her finger. "So...last night..."

"I know." Andi cleared her throat. "Do you hate me?"

"For what?" Kari took the phone away from her face long enough to give it a bewildered stare. Then she scrunched her eyes closed. Had things gone further than she'd thought after she'd bolted? "Wait, you didn't have sex with my guys, did you?"

What the hell had just come out of her mouth? Kari blushed, then quickly added, "Sorry. Don't answer that. It's none of my business and they're not *my guys*."

Andi laughed. "First, no. I swear. I didn't touch them. It was eye candy only. I mean, okay, I did see their cocks."

"You did?"

"Yeah, they, uhhhh, liked our show, I guess," Andi hedged.

"Are you telling me they masturbated while you guys fucked?" Kari wasn't pissed. In fact, she was squirming on her couch imagining it.

"Ford and Brady did. Josh disappeared." Andi went on in a rush, "I hardly saw anything, I swear. I was so busy with my guys, I wasn't really looking. Just enough to say that if they ever do become your guys—and I think they totally could if that's what you want—you'd be a *very* lucky woman."

"Oh. Well, I kissed Josh," Kari blurted, figuring she

owed it to Andi to come clean, too. "We were making out while you...you know."

"And then what?" Andi wondered.

"He took me home." Quick to correct any possible misunderstandings, she added, "Like dropped me off. Not, like, came in and slept with me."

"Too bad."

Was it? Kari still couldn't say. She felt strongly pulled in two polar opposite directions and they were tearing her apart. "I don't know, Andi. I don't want to lose my job. But I don't know if I can ignore the tension that seems to be building between us either."

"I don't think you have to choose one or the other." Andi sighed. "I get why that's awkward for you, though. If it comes down to it, I'm telling you, my department would love to have you."

"I guess I still have a lot of thinking to do before the weekend is over and I have to face them again." Kari rubbed her temple.

"I'll let you go so you can do that. But remember, I'm here if you need someone to talk to." Andi grew more serious then. "Thank you for understanding...about what happened. I swear to you it wasn't anything we'd planned and there weren't any boundaries crossed that would take away from you moving forward with Ford, Brady, and Josh. I really just wanted to say that to you woman to woman and not text it or something. I would hate myself if I accidentally fucked things up between you four. And, honestly, I really enjoyed hanging out with you last night."

"Not as much as you enjoyed what came after, I bet!" Kari snorted as Andi cracked up. She didn't blame the woman. If Kari had been the one at the center of that much prime attention, she'd feel the same way. That thought lingered as their laughter subsided.

Andi asked, "Maybe we could grab lunch sometime next week?"

"That would be great." Kari sighed. Usually she ended up eating with Ford, Brady, Josh or some combination of all three. "I might need a break from the guys and the office."

"I'm available every day. And even if I'm not, I'll make sure I am," Andi promised.

"Thank you." Kari disconnected the call, then stood up, restless. She roamed around her apartment from her living room through the kitchen and finally into her bedroom, where she eyed the drawer of her bedside table.

Maybe it was weird, but she couldn't help it. Andi's revelation had turned her on. Made her wish she'd been bolder and run into the captain's quarters instead of away from them the night before. Damn the consequences.

In real life, that wasn't a solid plan. But here, in the confines of her bedroom, she imagined what it might have been like.

Kari climbed into bed and took her vibrator from the drawer. She drew her T-shirt over her head, then wriggled out of her yoga pants.

By the time she had closed her eyes and started to imagine herself stumbling into the middle of Ford, Brady, and Josh, with their hands tucked in their pants as they watched the performance Andi and her guys were putting on for them.

*"Kari!" Ford barked, his eyes going wide.*

*"Looks like I'm just in time for the real festivities," she said, licking her lips as she strutted into the cabin instead of biting her tongue and fleeing.*

"Perfect timing," Brady agreed with a warm smile. "We're out of seats, though. Why don't you sit on the birthday boy's lap?"

Kari took him up on the offer, without hesitating or second-guessing her decision. It felt incredible to be so free and confident. Before she perched on him, she reached down and lifted the hem of her dress so she could straddle him properly with her back to his chest.

In front of them, Andi and her guys had progressed from foreplay to full-on intercourse. Reed was entering the other woman, raising the temperature in the intimate space and giving Kari the courage to take what she really wanted. Instead of wasting time on appetizers, she went straight for the main course.

Over her shoulder, she asked, "Why don't you take your cock out so we can catch up? They shouldn't have all the fun when it's your party."

"Good point." Ford grinned. He ripped open the front of his tux and exposed himself to her. He had a right to his prideful smirk. His cock was thick and long, and made her ache to have him inside her.

Kari slid her vibrator into her pussy as she imagined sheathing Ford, sliding down his length until she was settled fully in his lap.

"Damn, Kari," he rasped as he bit her neck lightly.

Meanwhile, Brady and Josh never once took their gazes off of her. She lifted a hand as though Ford wasn't stretching her, making her moan as he began to thrust upward from beneath her. She curled her fingers and beckoned them closer. In the background she could hear the grunts and sighs of Andi and her guys making love, showing Ford, Brady, Josh, and her what they were missing out on.

Kari didn't want to miss out anymore. She began to pump the vibrator inside her before turning it on low.

*Brady and Josh flew to her side, taking their dicks out too. Kari fisted Josh's length, pumping him in time to Ford's fucking. Brady put his hand on her cheek, cupping it and brushing his thumb across her lower lip until she knew exactly where he wanted to be.*

*She opened and took his cock inside, reveling in the heat and weight of him on her tongue.*

*Kari was full of them and the exhilaration they inspired inside her.*

*Pleasure as well.*

With a practiced flick, Kari sped up her toy, loving the way it felt as she imagined it was Ford. In real life, she had a feeling they would take things slow and make it last all night. But right then, there was no way her imagination was going to let her get away with that. Self-control had gone out the window the moment Andi had confessed what had happened.

*Kari gave herself over to them completely. Ford's hands wrapped around her waist and braced her as he continued his relentless thrusts. She ground over him, increasing the pressure of their bodies against each other where they fit together.*

*When she moaned, Brady gasped. The trill of her ecstasy traveled along his shaft, making precome leak from his tip. She devoured the fluid, enjoying his taste. Beside him, Josh groaned and his erection jerked in her fist.*

*His balls slapped the side of her hand as he fucked into it, never once taking his eyes off her and his partners in favor of the mounting noise from across the room.*

*When he reached down and squeezed her breast through her dress, she felt the first clench of her muscles around Ford's shaft.*

"Yes. Do that again, Josh." He cursed. "She's going to come all over my cock."

Kari muffled her scream with the back of her free hand. The other was working her vibrator in time to fantasy-Ford's fucking. She visualized what it would be like to unravel at their hands while she brought herself relief with her own.

In her mind she saw them falling too.

*Ford waited until she'd nearly squeezed him in half before joining her. The lingering clenches of her channel wrung him dry as he flooded her pussy with jet after jet of his come. Brady tugged on her hair and held her close to his abdomen as he did the same.*

*When Kari shifted her gaze to Josh, she watched him tip over the edge. He bulged in her hand, the veins on his cock growing even more defined, before his release poured over her knuckles.*

It took minutes for Kari to catch her breath. And when she did, she realized she hadn't fully satisfied herself despite coming hard enough to put her favorite tool in jeopardy. It took several more rounds and a fresh set of batteries to exorcise her illicit desires.

When she finally settled in to her bed and drifted toward sleep, she promised herself she'd go back to thinking about them strictly as her bosses by the time Monday morning rolled around. Otherwise, she was bound to make a fool out of herself at work, and likely lose her job in the process.

Because now that she'd allowed herself to dream about what life could be like if she was as bold as her new friends, it was going to be nearly impossible to unsee the possibilities.

## 10

By the time her alarm went off on Monday, Kari thought she might be able to act halfway normal around Ford, Brady, and Josh again. She had to. Risking her job wasn't in her plan, despite how reckless she'd been Friday night. It had taken the entire weekend for the impression of Josh's lips to fade from her mouth enough that she didn't find herself touching them and sighing at random intervals.

She buttoned her shirt until it nearly choked her and wound her bun tight enough that it gave her a mini-facelift before marching off to the bus stop. If she was sweating the entire ride into downtown, it was because she sported her thickest suit as if it were armor, not because she was freaking out over seeing her bosses.

Yeah, right.

Kari pasted on the professional yet not too friendly smile that she'd practiced in the mirror earlier, then stormed the polished elevator to the law firm. She was thrilled she'd gotten in early enough that she didn't have to make small talk with anyone as she scurried to her office and turned on her computer.

When Brady appeared at her doorway, clutching a cup of coffee as if he'd slept as little as she had the past few nights, he acted as though everything—including his atypical exhaustion—was normal.

They chatted for a few minutes about the party and how much fun they'd had before he let her know Josh had brought treats for the staff. Kari's guts unkinked slightly, enough that she might be able to choke down one of the muffins she could see Josh setting on the conference room table, on the other side of the glass wall from her office door. Employees began to mill about, trying to get into the groove after a couple days off.

Kari followed Brady as he headed for the refreshments, trying not to stare at his ass. If nothing else, a dose of sugar would help her survive the awkwardness that loomed. So she skipped the muffins and went straight to the hard stuff. Donuts.

She leaned her hip against the sleek table, nibbling on a jelly-filled-sprinkle-topped piece of heaven with her coworkers. Of course she was in the middle of licking icing off her fingertips when Ford ambled into the room.

His stride faltered as his gaze snapped to her mouth. For a moment, he seemed suspended there before resuming his march toward the pastries and coffee. "Good morning."

"Hey." She smiled, hoping she didn't have any stray jam on her face.

Kari wondered how much more intensely he'd been staring at Andi on Friday night than he was studying her right then. How had the other woman kept herself from melting between the embraces of her three lovers and the appreciation of a trio of even more incredible men?

Cooper distracted her from that line of thinking when he joined them with a fist pump. "Breakfast, nice."

"I thought Andi spoiled you by cooking for you every morning?" Ford asked with a shake of his head at their intern's enthusiasm.

"That's sort of true. We eat together as often as we can, though I'm usually the one who cooks for her if she'll let me. I'm always game for second breakfast." Cooper shrugged. "Especially if it's something less healthy than oatmeal or some of that fiber-filled cereal she's always trying to get us to eat."

"You'd think your girl wants to keep you around for a while or something." Brady laughed as he slapped Cooper on the back. "Have fun burning off all that extra energy later."

The comment might have seemed innocent enough if they hadn't shared the experience on the yacht a few days earlier. Kari's cheeks flamed and she nearly choked on her sip of coffee. "I'd better get back to work."

She brushed past Ford, ignoring the firmness of his biceps beneath his perfectly tailored suit, then hid behind her desk until much later that morning, when she couldn't avoid her bosses any longer. It was time for their weekly executive staff meeting.

No matter how hard it was, she focused on the job they paid her to do instead of what they had looked like relaxed and partying on their yacht. Two hours flew by as they got their plan in order and discussed case after case. As their reputations had grown, so did their workload. Soon they were going to need to hire more lawyers, if they planned to keep taking on more clients.

Maybe even increase the size of her administrative staff. Kari reviewed her notes and wondered how she would get through everything by the end of the month, never mind the week. Then again, she didn't mind more overtime since Ford, Brady, and Josh had been flexible with her. She sighed as she remembered shopping for the dress they'd treated her to and how scared she'd been that she'd pushed her luck.

With their plan of attack in place, she and the guys slid back from the table, ready to put their heads down and get some shit done like the high-functioning team they'd become. Before she could think better of it, she exclaimed, "I'm so glad things are…normal-ish."

Ford took off his reading glasses and laid them neatly on the table in front of him. The staccato deliberateness of the gesture put her on high alert.

Josh blinked at her, as if shocked she'd breached their unspoken vow not to mention what had happened. She probably should have kept her mouth shut. But the revelation made her nearly giddy. She hadn't realized how much working with them meant to her until she'd feared she'd have to give it up.

"As opposed to what?" Brady tipped his head, the rest of his body staying stock still. He scanned her expression as if searching for clues.

"Weird." She shrugged. "You know, after the party. And what happened at the end of the night…"

"Why should things be awkward?" Ford peered at her. "We're all consenting adults here. Andi was fine with it too. She said she doesn't care that you know what was happening down below."

"I know, we talked," Kari admitted.

"You did? That's great." Josh smiled. "We just hope

that *you're* okay with everything, and that it didn't upset you."

"Me? I'm fine." More than fine, really. It was liberating that things could be the same as they had been before. That she hadn't doomed herself to another prickly situation day after day because she'd attended the party or because she was still a slave to her past.

"Thank God. I've been worried sick all weekend, but it seemed hypocritical to call you just to ask if you wanted us to keep our distance." Brady pressed his fingers to his temple as if he'd had a massive tension headache, like she knew he sometimes got during rough times at the office. His shoulders slumped enough that she realized just how wound up he'd been.

*They'd* been concerned about *her*? That told her everything she needed to know about them.

Marty had never given a fuck about how uncomfortable he made her. In fact, he'd gotten off on it, she was pretty sure. Relief rushed through her, transforming her bones to limp noodles and—apparently —loosening her lips further as well.

She glanced over her shoulder toward the doorway to make sure no one else on staff discovered her indiscretion. First Marty, now another boss—a partner this time. Her reputation couldn't handle another blow like that. People would assume she was trying to sleep her way to the top. Hell, a few of them already did.

Then, quietly, she asked, "So...you really don't care that I made out with Josh?"

"You *what*?" Ford blinked at her a few times, as if he hadn't heard her clearly. His fingers curled around his pen and his knuckles turned white. She was afraid he was going to snap the thing in half.

"Josh? Is that true?" Brady spun his chair toward his friend and glared. Intense in any situation, he practically bored holes in the other guy then.

*Oh shit.* Kari's eyes bulged as she whipped her guilty stare first to Josh then to Brady and, finally, to Ford. The tiny sliver of jealousy and—was that disappointment?—she saw there ripped her to shreds.

They hadn't known after all. No wonder things had seemed okay.

And this was *exactly* why she shouldn't have indulged in that kiss. That perfect, amazing, soul-crushing meeting of mouths. The one she'd wished she could have experienced over and over every moment since she'd stopped it and fled from Josh's arms.

Because it had the power to ruin everything. Not only her career, but their friendship as well. After what she'd heard from them the day they'd fired Marty, and what she'd seen on the boat, she thought it wouldn't have been a big deal. That they would have discussed it together.

Instead, Josh had kept what they'd done a dirty little secret from his partners.

Kari stood up so fast, she knocked her chair over in the process. Josh lunged forward and caught it, righting it before it could make a clatter that would draw curious coworkers.

She had to get out of there before she made a fool of herself in front of them. Again.

"I'm taking the rest of the day off. I understand if you don't want me to come back tomorrow. Just...email me or something." Kari was proud she kept her shit together as she rushed through the frosted glass of their entryway toward the secured elevator. It required a keycard to access the top-level offices, which had made her feel better since Marty had threatened her on his way out, kicking a hole in her office door.

Today it only made her realize how much that one stolen kiss might end up costing her—access to the part of her life she valued most and the three men who made it so rewarding to work for them.

"Kari, wait up! Are you okay?" It wasn't one of her three bosses checking on her. No, they were about to break into a full-on fistfight from the sounds of the shouting behind her.

It was Cooper.

"Hey, calm down. Take a deep breath." He approached slowly and held his hand out.

"I can't." Kari rocked herself as darkness encroached.

"You can," he said kindly, gently. "The elevator is almost here. Keep your shit together until we get in it, then you can unload."

The sound of other people checking to see what the ruckus was reached into Kari's whirling mind. She jammed her hand out and latched onto Cooper's wrist. He steadied her and ushered her into the car that opened up in front of them.

"Thank you," she choked out before crumpling against the cool metal.

"No problem." He grimaced. "What the hell happened back there? Was it because of...us?"

"Of course not." Kari groaned. She didn't want anyone else to feel judged like she had so often. "It's just...complicated."

"Would you feel better talking to Andi about it? She won't say anything to me you don't want her to. She's a great listener, and I think maybe she might understand what you're going through." He already had his phone in his hand. "Did you know we were roommates for four years before we became more? It was...scary. And we almost lost her as even a friend before we figured out how to make things work between us. But I promise you, it can be done. If that's what you want. All of you, I mean."

Kari bit her lip to keep it from trembling. Her insides ached and she admitted it...she was terrified. For her future, and for her bosses and the friendship they'd built over the years.

Things were changing and maybe none of them were ready for how much.

"Yeah. Could you do that? Call her?" Kari asked.

"Of course. Better yet, I'll take you to our place and ask her to meet us there for a long lunch if you want." He lifted the phone to his ear. A few moments later, he was already talking.

Before Kari could tell him that was too much trouble to go to for her, he'd already arranged everything. It meant a lot to have friends to help her work through this. After Marty, she'd closed herself off from even casual acquaintances except for her guarded rapport with Ford, Brady, and Josh.

Maybe she'd had it all wrong.

Maybe she should have opened up instead of hiding herself away. If she had, today could have gone a lot differently. Kari was confused. Shocked. A thousand times more worried than she'd been on her way to work that morning. Her chest ached.

She watched the office building until it disappeared through the window of the cab Cooper had called for them. Hopefully, speaking with Andi would help clear her mind so she could figure out what to do about the colossal mess her life had become.

## 11

"What the fuck did you do?" Ford took a step forward, and then another, like he might actually lunge at Josh or take a swing at his face.

Josh didn't try to dodge. He deserved an ass beating. "I screwed up."

"Yeah, I'd say so." Brady crossed his arms over his chest. Usually the easier of the two to get along with, he didn't seem to be giving Josh any wiggle room at the moment.

Josh felt like one of the poor bastards Brady was known to crush on cross-examination. "Look, she kissed me. And I didn't know what to do. I didn't want to reject her or make her feel like she did something wrong..."

"Come on. That's bullshit. And even if that was the whole truth, that's exactly what ended up happening anyway just now. Because you didn't come clean to us about your secret tonsil hockey match, she thinks we're upset with her instead of your lying ass." Ford threw up his hands. "Fuck, man. I wouldn't have blamed you for making out with her, or more, you know that. If she wants you, that's fine. It just…"

"Caught us off guard." Brady nodded solemnly, his shoulders slumping then.

"Makes me jealous as fuck, too," Ford snarled. "No wonder you weren't pissed at us for staying to watch Andi and her guys."

"You acted like some kind of martyr when really you were stabbing us in the back. Fuck, Josh. I didn't think you had that in you." Brady's disappointment was way worse than Ford's fury.

"I'm sorry, guys. Really." Josh scrunched his eyes closed for a moment. As shitty as it felt to be on the wrong side of his friends, it also felt so much better now that they knew what had really happened. If they were going to try for a relationship like the one Andi, Cooper, Reed, and Simon had, they had to be absolutely transparent with each other. He could see that now. So he forged ahead. "It freaked me out, that's all. It was the best damn kiss of my life and I wanted so much more, but it was obvious she didn't and…"

He clamped his jaw shut when his voice grew rough.

"You were devastated." Brady looked up then, his face smoothing out. "Son of a bitch, Josh. I'm sorry. You really should have told us. We could have at least knocked back some beers and talked about what to do next."

"I know. It was stupid. But I also didn't want to break the bad news to you guys. She's not ready for us. No matter how much we wish she was." He flopped into a chair then, unable to keep himself standing a moment longer. "Maybe she never will be either."

"We can deal with that. As long as she's okay." Ford looked out his window as if he wished he could blast through the glass like a superhero and fly wherever she was.

"I saw Cooper walking out with her. He'll make sure she gets home." Brady groaned. "Then we're going to have to figure out how to get her back here. Make sure she's comfortable and knows that nothing that's happened lately impacts what we think of her when we're at work."

Josh nodded. The look on her face that morning, the nervous tapping of her fingers and the tight slash of her lush lips during their meeting, had been eating at him the whole time. At least now he could address it with her and make sure she knew how appreciated she was.

From now on he wasn't going to be hiding anything from anyone. He'd share his feelings and handle how they impacted the people around him head-on. Maybe someday that would be enough to convince Kari he was serious about her. If it wasn't, he'd accept that too.

"Whether it's Kari or someone else, I think we can all agree on one thing: we haven't really accomplished all our goals. Or maybe we found a new one. Either way..." Ford turned to his desk, scribbled something on a Post-it Note and then held it out for Brady and Josh to see. "We've got more work to do."

*Convince the woman of our dreams to spend the rest of her life being worshipped by us.*

*Live the rest of our lives satisfied and happy.*

Josh whooped at that. Brady chuckled, but a slow smile spread across his face and erased some of the tension around his eyes. Ford marched to the framed checklist Brady had given him for his birthday and smooshed the neon yellow note at the bottom.

Knowing they were all in alignment and ready to

make it a reality dissolved some of the acid in his gut. When they worked together, nothing was impossible.

Before they could start formulating a plan to make their dream come true, Ford's phone rang. The fact that the call came through when Kari wasn't there to screen it meant whoever was contacting them was someone with Ford's direct number. There weren't many people who had it.

He looked at Josh and then Brady before lunging for it.

"Hello? Hey, Andi, hang on a second. Can I put you on speaker?" Ford asked as he scrubbed his hand over his face, then punched a few buttons. "Brady and Josh are here with me. Go ahead."

"Why is Kari on her way here? Cooper called and said she needed to talk to me. I could hear her in the background. She sounded upset. Is it because of Friday night?" Andi sounded distraught herself. Damn, they were hurting people they cared about. The people they least wanted to offend.

"Yes," Ford admitted.

"Shit!" Andi's voice wavered. "Does she think less of me for it? I called her and I thought we were cool—"

"What?" Brady shook his head and Josh rushed to correct her.

"No, Andi. It's not you. It's us. No, *me*. It's my fault. I sort of made out with her and didn't tell the guys..."

"Josh!" Andi shrieked. "That's so stupid!"

"I know, I know." And he did. Now. He should have been upfront and prevented all this.

"You guys are never going to make this work if you're not completely open. With each other and the girl you want."

"Is it that obvious?" Brady groaned.

"Ummmm, yup. Pretty much." Andi laughed then, her tension evaporating as she turned her attention to matchmaking. Josh wasn't above using any help they could get to work through this.

"So what would you suggest?" Brady asked. "We want to show her we're serious but make sure she knows the choice is hers and independent of anything that happens here at the firm."

"Here's what I'll do. I'll try to show her there's no reason for concern until she can discuss this with you guys in person. I'll vouch for you again if you swear you're going to get your shit together. And soon." Andi sighed. "I can see where the office isn't the right place for these discussions. It's already your home field. If I were her, I'd be uncomfortable there with all this hanging over my head. What about tomorrow morning? Before work? Would you be willing to meet up with her then and hash this out before you make the same mistake again tomorrow? It's not right to stress her out like that at her job. If Cooper can tell something's up, so can everyone else you work with."

Ford nodded. "Yeah, you're right. If Josh hadn't been a fucking idiot, we would have taken care of it already."

Josh winced, but it was true. "There's a diner down the street she loves that has amazing breakfast food, the Over Easy. We can be there at six, if she'll agree to talk to us. *If.* Seriously, make sure she knows that no matter how she feels, we will understand and accept that."

"Damn straight you will." Andi huffed.

"Thank you, Andi," Brady said. "We owe you. Big time."

"You do. But more than that...you owe yourselves this chance. You're great people and you deserve to be happy.

Don't screw it up just because you're afraid it might be too good to be true or because you think you know what Kari needs without asking her directly."

"You're awfully smart for your age," Ford teased.

"Just be there tomorrow, Gramps. And be ready to give her everything or move on." Andi turned stern then. "I like her. I like you. I could see the chemistry between you at the party the other day. I don't want anyone to get hurt...worse. Figure this shit out."

"Yes, ma'am." Ford's lips kicked up in a smirk as he disconnected the phone. Then he turned to Brady and Josh. "You heard the lady."

"You guys are really ready for this?" Josh asked. He had to be sure, because if he got his hopes up again only to have them smashed, he wasn't sure he'd survive.

"We all are. It's time to admit what we've been heading toward for a while. This is what you guys want, right?" Ford straightened his sleeves, tugging on the ends until the lines of his jacket were straight and crisp. No nonsense.

"It is," Brady agreed.

"Yeah." Josh nodded.

"Then let's get to work." Ford opened the top folder on his desk. "If we knock out our caseload for the day, we can go home and spend tonight figuring out exactly what we want to say tomorrow. If we only get one chance to make our case, I want to do it right."

For the first time since Friday, Josh took a deep breath.

"So just tell me one thing before we get started..." Brady said to Josh as he leaned forward.

"Yeah?"

"How good was it?"

"Incredible." He had to spread his legs wider as

pleasure washed over him at the memory. "Dangerous. I'd give up everything we've worked for to do it again."

"If we hadn't gotten to watch Andi and her guys while you were busy getting addicted to Kari, I'd have to knock that smirk off your face right now." Ford growled. "I guess we're even."

Josh figured it was best not to correct the guy. Ford didn't need to know just how much better Josh's evening had been than theirs. If they were lucky, they'd find out soon enough.

And if they weren't, at least he'd be the only one suffering.

## 12

Ford leaned up against the wall near the door of the diner Josh had sworn Kari drooled over. Of course he would know. He paid attention to little shit like that.

The smell of eggs and bacon made Ford's stomach rumble. Or was thinking about how today might end that had him desperately *hungry*?

This was either the best or worst decision they'd ever made. But he felt it. They were at a crossroads. How they handled this situation could break the three—no, *four*—of them apart. And that certainly included sitting back and doing nothing. So he'd have to act. In the most cautious and careful way he knew how, because if Kari got hurt due to their artless fumbling around, trying to figure out how to make this work, he'd never forgive himself.

Their friendship and their partnership would crumble.

For the first time, Ford acknowledged that meant something to him. More than simply for the pursuit of success or the epic quenching of their lust, he'd gotten used to having Brady and Josh in his world. They had an everyday routine—at home and at work. Their lives were irrevocably entwined. He wasn't sure when it had happened exactly, but sometime in the past decade, they'd grown into a single high-performing unit.

Losing at love meant demolishing that foundation, too.

He wasn't sure he could handle rebuilding from scratch and certainly didn't want to in any case.

When he spotted the bounce of gorgeous, long auburn waves through the plate-glass window, he stood at attention. Was that some sort of code? Was she prepared to see them as something other than her employers? Unfortunately, when Kari pressed through the strangers surrounding her, her infectious smile was nowhere to be seen.

Oh shit, maybe he should send her away and pretend like this hadn't happened. Josh and Brady would never forgive him if he did. There was too much at stake not to fight for what they really needed.

Ford crossed to the door and opened it for Kari, ushering her inside. "Good morning."

"Hey." She didn't flinch or run, so he figured that was a decent start. When she tipped her face up and breathed deep of the warm vanilla and strawberry scent permeating the place, she hummed. "They have the best waffles here. At least if we have to have an awkward conversation, we might as well do it over good food."

Biting his tongue lest he say something about rather having *her* for breakfast, Ford nodded and extended his arm. Not because he thought of her differently today, but because he was always as much of a gentleman as he could pretend to be around her. A gentleman with a bit of a possessive, protective streak. If she was going to accept their proposal, it was better that she saw each of them for who they really were.

She leaned into his hold instead of away from it, so he didn't retract his light touch on her lower back as he steered her toward the table where Josh and Brady were eagerly waiting. They'd thought it best not to overwhelm her right up front. Besides, the place was packed. If they hadn't grabbed a table when they first arrived—obscenely early—for their meeting, they wouldn't have any place to sit now.

Another win for teamwork.

When they approached, Brady stood. Josh did his best to follow suit from his place deeper in the booth.

"Thank you for coming," Brady said, his eyes trained on their guest.

"Kari..." was all Josh could say.

It was enough. That one word was so filled with longing and anguish, Kari had to realize he felt like shit for unintentionally hurting her.

She nodded, blinking a few times as she looked away, over her shoulder. Ford couldn't help but tighten his hold, hugging her to his side briefly before helping her settle into the booth. He scooted in after her, not at all sad that her thigh stayed pressed to his where they sat.

While he was distracted, Josh and Brady were exchanging glances, figuring out what to say. Ford left them to it. They were better communicators than he could ever be. He was more of an action man himself.

"First, I just want to say sorry." Josh fiddled with the napkin-wrapped silverware in front of him.

"For what?" Kari tipped her head, her eyes narrowing.

*Uh oh. Danger zone.* "For kissing me? Or for forgetting to tell them that it happened?"

"What do you want me to apologize for?" Josh wondered. "I mostly feel bad for how things turned out yesterday. I should have handled it better to avoid making you uncomfortable at work."

Ford was certain that bastard didn't regret a moment of the time his lips had spent on hers. Asking him to lie about that wouldn't solve their problems.

"Does that mean the three of you are fighting? Because of me?" Kari's face seemed paler than usual then. As if that was her worst fear, unlike some women, who would have reveled in having that sort of sway over them. That wasn't why she was asking. She cared about them more than she wanted them. He would have to remember to treat her with the same respect, no matter how badly he desired her.

"Not exactly," Ford was quick to reassure her. He slipped into lawyer mode. "If I had another chance to react to what happened, I would have asked how you feel about what Josh did. It just caught me by surprise, that's all."

"To be fair, Josh didn't really do anything. It just sort of happened. He was comforting me. We both... participated." Kari sighed, and Josh attempted to smother a strangled groan behind his napkin.

That lucky bastard.

"Either way, how do you feel about it?" Brady asked with a quiet sternness that Ford knew meant he was serious as fuck. They had so much riding on her response. So many hopes and dreams. The way Josh held his breath and leaned in made Ford certain he was dying to hear the answer himself.

"Confused, I guess." Kari's shoulders slumped and she leaned back against the booth's padded cushion.

"That's understandable." Ford nodded.

"I mean, it was pretty much the best kiss of my life."

Josh perked up.

"But..."

Josh froze.

"If it messed everything else up, I'm not sure it was worth it. Sorry." She looked at Josh then, wincing. "I love my job. I love the challenge of keeping the office running as smoothly as possible. I love watching the three of you work together. I love spending time with you. I love—"

Brady looked as if he might beg her to finish her thought. Ford kicked his shin. They'd agreed not to hound her if she wasn't ready to move forward, no matter how badly they craved her. They'd wait if she needed more time to get used to the new direction they seemed headed in. Or surrender gracefully if she decided it wasn't for her at all.

Josh reached out and laid his hand, palm up, on the table in front of her. "I promise you, you didn't mess anything up. Okay?"

She bit her lower lip, then nodded tentatively. "Okay."

Jealousy seared up Ford's spine in a white-hot flash when Kari put her hand in Josh's. Only for a second, though. Because then she turned to him and Brady with a gorgeous smile. One even more brilliant than the one he'd grown used to seeing every day. She said, "In that case, it was a-*fucking*-mazing and I wouldn't mind doing it again a thousand times or so."

Brady put his water glass on the table too hard. Droplets sloshed over the rim. Ford could relate; he was barely keeping his instincts restrained. If it wasn't for the other two guys chaperoning him, he'd probably have followed Josh's lead and kissed Kari senseless by now.

Except she hadn't said she was interested in that, only in making out with Josh some more.

Josh noticed their tension. He cleared his throat, then asked what Ford was dying to know. "I'm so glad to hear that, Kari. Seriously. But...what about these two? What if we are a package deal? You heard our confession to Cooper..."

Her skin began to turn pink from the tops of her breasts, which were revealed by the V-neck of her light sweater, then up her neck and cheeks. It only made her look more attractive. "I did."

"And?" Brady prodded. "It's a lot, I know. If you're only into Josh, we get that. Neither Ford nor I would begrudge him happiness. But...how does it make you feel to know that we're interested in sharing?"

"Hot." Her response was instantaneous. It was only one word, but it was the most incredible word Ford had ever heard in his life. Better yet, Kari lifted her gaze and met each of theirs in turn so they could see the desire blazing in her gorgeous eyes.

There might still be some hope for them.

If they handled things right from here on out.

"There's just one thing..." She swallowed hard.

"What's that?" Ford asked. Anything. She could ask them for a million dollars or to run down the street naked and they'd do their best to grant her wishes. He already knew they hadn't had a chance like this before. One that could turn into a real relationship with someone all three of them cared deeply for.

"I've been chatting with Andi." She smiled. "She's really great. Cooper, Reed, and Simon got lucky with her."

The guys all nodded. Ford remembered how she'd looked, coming apart at their touches. Kari hadn't seen anything yet. But maybe she could learn for herself.

"Anyway, one thing I'm sure of is that I want something like they have. Each of them has a strong relationship outside of the things they share together. You know, sex. And their intimate relationship." Kari cleared her throat. "I feel like the most spoiled woman alive saying this, but…I'd like that, too. To come to know and care for each of you independently as well as all of you together."

"That's no problem," Ford said instantly. He didn't even have to look at Brady or Josh to be sure they would agree. In fact, there was some selfish part of him that loved the possibility of having her to himself sometimes. To show her what kind of man he could be with her by his side.

"That's exactly what we want, too," Brady reassured her.

Josh smiled. "It's great to have people you can count on in any situation and ones who have your back all the time. These guys are my best friends and business partners. But I want whoever we end up with to love me for me and not just me because I come along with the package, you know?"

Ford could hear what Josh didn't say. There'd been plenty of women who pursued them for their status or wealth. With Kari, they knew that wasn't an issue. She knew them. Really knew them. And if she chose them, it wouldn't be for what they had, but what they could give her aside from material possessions.

"So I guess all that's left is to ask who you want to take you out on a date first." Ford grinned then. "I'm handsomest. I think it should be me."

"I'm oldest." Brady laughed while Josh snorted.

"I'm fine with being last since I sort of already had a sneak peek." Josh wiggled his brows so Kari knew he was only teasing.

She cracked up along with them. "I don't care about that. You guys figure it out. All I want to know is...where's the damn menu? I need to order a big breakfast if I'm going to keep up with the three of you."

Ford knew she didn't mean it like it sounded, but inside, the crude portion of his brain cheered her on. Brady choked on his water and Josh grinned for a moment before he got more serious.

"Thank you, Kari. For giving us this chance. I promise we'll do our best not to fuck it up. And no matter what, I swear that nothing that happens between us will ever spill over into the office again." Josh squeezed her fingers lightly and Kari seemed to melt. She relaxed, the tension in her leg fleeing, allowing it to press more fully against Ford's.

"Okay." She nodded. "I'm holding you to that. It's bad enough that everyone knows about Marty. If they found out about us dating, it would make them think I was trying to sleep my way to the top for sure. I couldn't handle that."

Ford reared back. He hadn't quite thought of it in that way, but he could understand why that would sting. She'd earned every bit of her authority at the firm. Her capableness was one of the things that attracted him to her, in fact.

"Fuck what anyone else thinks. We know the truth." He frowned as Josh and Brady glowered at him. Things were going too well for him to rock the boat now. So he held his hands up in front of him. "But fine. I agree. Everything will be business as usual at work."

She nodded and beamed up at him.

"But when I pick you up for our date? All bets are off."

Her gaze turned ravenous, and not for fucking waffles either. Without thought, he gave in to his instincts and swooped down to steal a taste of her. If Brady hadn't been there, clearing his damn throat, it might have turned into a hell of a lot more than a quick buss.

Even that was enough to convince him that whatever happened next had the power to change their lives forever. He prayed it would be for the better.

## 13

L eading up to her date with Ford, it had been difficult for Kari to imagine anything could top the glamour and fun of the birthday bash on his yacht.

All week at work, things had been relatively normal. The guys had kept their word. Nothing had changed when it came to her job. Well, nothing except how much time she spent dying of anticipation and wondering what it would be like to spend time with them outside the boundaries she'd laid down and strictly enforced.

And now she knew.

A date with Ford might not have been as carefree as dancing in the moonlight with Josh or as elegant as engaging conversation with Brady, but it was intimate as fuck.

No, seriously, dinner had proved to be more intense than sleeping with some of her previous lovers. Because sharing the decadent food with him in the candlelight at the city's most exclusive restaurant left nowhere to hide from his piercing gaze. He held her hand between courses, driving her mad with the brush of his thumb over her knuckles.

He was strong. He was fiercely protective.

And she'd be lying if she said that those qualities weren't a turn on.

Ford made her feel secure, enough that comfort began to seep into her better sense and free all these pent-up emotions she'd been suppressing at work. She could finally express them to him while they waited for their desserts to arrive.

"You know, I've wanted—for a long time now—to say thank you properly." Kari bit her lip in an attempt to keep it from quivering as she escalated their chatter between bites from polite to serious.

"Huh? For what?" He leaned forward, only increasing his focus on her. For a man who lived and breathed intensity, that was a lot to take. He brought his other hand up to the table and laid it over their clasped ones so that he enfolded her fingers entirely in his hands.

It was comforting to know he would shelter her the same way if she needed it. And she might after she laid herself bare.

"For everything you did after the situation with Marty." She glanced over his shoulder toward the window and the street beyond. It was dark now. Late. Traffic had dwindled. Only a few people scurried by in the rain that had evolved from drizzle to downpour while they ate.

"I didn't do nearly enough." The strain in his sexy voice snapped her stare back to him.

"How can you say that?" She gaped at him. "You were there for me. Held my hand—like this—when I gave my statement to the police. You ran interference so I wouldn't have to interact with him at the firm until you finally figured out a way to remove him permanently from my world. Without that and Josh pulling me out of my black moods and Brady talking me off the ledge when things seemed overwhelming....well, I'm not sure where I'd be today."

She stopped short of admitting how lost she'd been and how she had considered, in the darkest moments, doing something stupid and rash. Harming herself. Until she had remembered Ford telling her that anything that hurt her, hurt him, too.

She couldn't do that to him.

Whatever they'd called it before—and whatever they were going to call it from here on out—there had always been something between them. Something powerful that had lent her strength when she needed it most.

Kari would never forget that.

"I should have stopped it so you didn't need us to do any of those things afterward. It kills me to know what happened to you right under our noses." Ford swallowed hard, then said in a rush, "I've never felt like more of a failure than when we realized what he did to you. I'm so sorry I didn't protect you and that we didn't react more quickly so we could have prosecuted him for his crimes. I can't believe you're even giving me this chance tonight after I blew it so bad. I never thought this would happen."

Her guts twisted. Had he been living with misplaced guilt? Just like she had been? Seeing Ford beat himself up unlocked something deep inside her. His self-torture was like a mirror, reflecting her own.

She would never again let what had happened make her criticize herself or her actions.

It hadn't been her fault. And it sure as shit hadn't been Ford's.

"Hey. I need you to do me a favor, okay?"

"Anything."

"Don't give him the power to fuck shit up between us." Kari grinned as Ford blinked at her.

"You know, it always surprises me when you say stuff like that." Ford smiled, too.

"Why? That's how I always talk."

"I know, and I like it. I guess because I hoped that somewhere inside you there was a dirty girl who might like to come out and play with us."

"Oh. Well, I guess you got your wish then." She continued now that she'd lightened the mood a shade or two. "But I'm serious. Marty has taken enough things from me already. I never want the way he made us feel—you, me, Brady, and Josh—to come between us. I suspect it has been keeping us apart despite..."

Ford cleared his throat. "Despite what?"

"Our attraction." She dared him to deny it.

He didn't.

Ford reached for his ice water and took several large, uncouth gulps before returning his full attention to her. "I'm glad I'm not the only one who feels this."

Kari fanned her face, wondering when it had gotten so warm inside the restaurant.

"You're right, of course. He's had too much power over us all. That ends tonight. Right now." Ford squeezed her hand, then let his fingers roam up her wrist. The contact sent a zing of electricity along her nerves, straight to her heart.

Who knew where it might have continued to if the waiter hadn't approached right then with an ornate silver tray. "Here we have the chocolate raspberry mousse dome and the warm pear tarte with almond frangipane, pistachio ice cream, and a trio of coulis."

Kari's eyes went wide as he set the most delicious-looking desserts she'd ever seen in front of them. Despite being stuffed, she was going to make some room for hers and, hopefully a nibble or two of Ford's as well.

Her eyes closed and she hummed as she forked the first bite into her mouth.

"I could watch you eat that all night." Ford groaned. "In fact...here, try some of mine."

He scooped up some of his and held it out to her. Who was she to argue? He knew the way to her heart, and she wasn't ashamed of it either.

Kari leaned forward and wrapped her lips around his silverware, sucking it clean as he withdrew.

A muscle ticced in Ford's jaw.

This could be fun. Kari grinned as she licked stray chocolate from her lips, enjoying teasing the man across from her. It seemed impossible that she could have that big of an impact on him, but he was riveted to her every move.

It was probably because of her intense preoccupation with his appreciative stare that she didn't see the man outside until he shattered their peace with a sudden, loud bang on the glass with both fists. Kari jumped in her seat, her gaze whipping to the intruder.

He was wearing a dirty black coat. His hair was scraggly and much longer than she remembered. Still, she knew that face. Knew that mean snarl. It triggered a flashback so intense she forgot where she was and who she was with. A groan wrenched from her chest as the dessert she'd been so enjoying threatened to choke her.

*Marty*!

Kari felt the blood drain from her face. Her heart skipped a few beats then made up for it by racing afterwards. She stood so suddenly, her chair tipped as her hands flew to her chest to try to keep her pounding heart inside it.

Before she could turn and flee, Ford rushed to her side, sliding from his chair like a sleek panther in his dark suit. Without hesitation, he enveloped her in his arms, tucking her against his broad, muscled chest as he angled himself so that he was between her and the window. She buried her cheek against his warmth, rubbing her face on his shirt and breathing deep of his familiar, calming scent.

Of course, she'd never been quite this close to him before.

Now that she was, she didn't want to break apart. It didn't matter who was outside so long as Ford was here. He wouldn't let anyone hurt her. As the realization sank in, she was able to put more weight on her jellified legs. Her arms went around him and she smothered him in a bear hug to help keep herself upright.

"Are you okay?" he asked quietly. "Some asshole was getting his jollies from pounding on the glass, scaring people having a nice time. That's all. Probably jealous that I'm having dinner with the most gorgeous woman in the city tonight."

He stroked her hair until she started to forget about being terrified.

Kari nodded, squeezing her eyes shut against the tricks her mind had played. In that moment, she'd thought she'd seen a ghost.

"Sorry. It must have been our conversation." She shook her head, then peered up at Ford. She might as well be honest so that he knew she was still—and probably always would be—a little fucked up. He deserved to know what he was signing up for. "I thought...for a second, I thought it was Marty."

Ford grasped her tighter then. Instead of telling her she was crazy, he signaled to the maître d'. He held her close as he murmured direct instructions without disclosing why it was so urgent and embarrassing her further. The staff, of course, took him seriously. After all, he was one of the wealthiest and most influential men in the city. If he wasn't happy here, their business would suffer.

Two waiters took off into the night, scouring the street outside their window thoroughly before returning to report to their boss. The man approached them as Ford continued to hold her and sway on his feet, gently rocking her into calmness.

"I'm sorry, Mr. Westbrook," the maître d' apologized. "They weren't able to find anyone matching your description. I apologize that your dinner was ruined. It's on the house tonight."

"Let's get out of here, okay?" Ford whispered before glancing at the table and their spoiled desserts, shaking his head before meeting her gaze to see what she wanted to do.

Kari had lost her appetite, but she'd rather go back to the table and choke down her final course than go home alone, feeling like she did right then. So she didn't agree. Or say anything at all.

Of course, Ford knew the exact thing to do. He met the maître d's stare and said, "Thank you. Would you let my driver know we're ready to go?"

"Of course, sir." The man nodded, then headed for his

station while speaking into the headset that kept him in contact with the rest of his staff.

"We'll ride around, locked in the car, until you feel steady again. Bronson won't let anyone follow us. Okay?" Ford took one hand from Kari's shoulder to fish his wallet out. Despite the offer of a freebie, he slipped out enough hundred dollar bills to cover their check twice over and laid them on the table. Then he steered her toward the front of the restaurant and away from the curious stares of the people around them.

It drew enough attention being on Ford Westbrook's arm. Never mind causing a scene on top of it. Kari kept her head ducked until they reached the atrium. Had she been foolish to think she belonged with a man like him?

Some of the judgmental looks she caught in her peripheral vision said yes.

Maybe it was best that reality had crashed her fairytale evening before she forgot that she was better suited to pumpkins and TV dinners than limos and gourmet fare.

## 14

Lights reflected off the wet black pavement as they zipped through traffic in the backseat of the limo. Bronson whisked them away from the restaurant in a circuitous route that made Ford sure the man hadn't blown off Kari's account of what had happened back at the restaurant. The guy seemed to have a soft spot for her, too, which meant he was thorny as hell when it came to anyone who might upset her.

If the person who had shattered their serene meal was more than just some random wacko—maybe someone Ford or his partners had put in jail or even Marty himself, though Ford didn't really think that was likely—Bronson made sure they wouldn't be able to tail the limo and figure out where Kari lived. As much as that should reassure Ford, it didn't seem like enough as they snaked their way across the city and closer to her home.

How would he let her go into her dark, empty apartment knowing how petrified she'd been, and probably still was? Regardless of what hadn't actually happened, in her mind, she'd gone to a terrifying place.

The pinched lines of her mouth as she quietly stared out at the buildings surrounding them convinced him she hadn't entirely shaken off the effects of that visit to hell either.

"What do you think about going back to our place for a drink?" Not only was Kari obviously rattled from what she'd thought she'd seen back at the restaurant, it gave Ford indigestion to know that he'd hoarded her for himself all evening. Things felt...off. Spiraling out of control from the perfect evening they'd been sharing just an hour ago. He didn't want it to end this way.

"You want me to spend some time with Brady and Josh?" Kari asked. She turned to face him. He held out his hand and she placed hers in it. So trusting, even now. So affectionate and perceptive. Willing to accommodate the needs of those she cared for.

Of course she understood.

Besides, it was a convenient—if legitimate—reason for her to stay with them a little longer. Protected and reassured that whatever fluke had destroyed dessert wasn't something she needed to worry about.

"I think it's important for them to know that after tonight I still feel the same as I did before our date." He lifted her hand and kissed the back of her knuckles. "I have a connection with you. At least it feels that way to me. Always has. It's getting stronger now. I respect that they have one, too. To be honest, I'm afraid that our date and how happy I am could lead to conflict between us. I hate fighting with those fuckers. If you swing by for a few, it might keep someone from getting a black eye."

Kari laughed, the soft sound wrapping around him in the darkness. It did things to him. And to his cock. But he was trying to ignore that for now and take things slow. He would hate for her to think he was another Marty in the making. "Then how can I say no?"

"You have a choice, Kari. With us, you're the one in charge."

"What if I don't want to be? Not always." She shrugged one bared shoulder and looked out the window at the cars flying by and the people who were still roaming the city streets despite the late hour and dank weather.

"Then that's fine, too." Ford's spirit stretched, rattling the bars of the cage he'd locked it into. He couldn't resist trailing a finger over the soft skin revealed by the sleeveless dress she wore. It was softer than he'd imagined. He never wanted to stop stroking her. "I promise we'll take care of you. Nothing will happen that you're not totally into."

She nodded. "Take me home, Ford."

*Fuck yes.*

## 15

Kari gasped softly as they exited the penthouse elevator. She knew where Ford, Brady, and Josh lived, of course. It was one thing to google the address and use image search to do a bit of friendly internet snooping on them, and another to be here in the flesh.

Dear God, the place was gorgeous. Stark white and silver everywhere, but without being cold. Fancier than she could have imagined in her wildest dreams. And lately she'd been having plenty of those.

Bright marble floors clicked beneath her heels as she walked beside Ford down the hall. They had no trouble fitting side by side, holding hands as they neared the enormous wall of windows she could see in the distance.

"So...how jealous do we need to be right now?" Brady called from around the corner.

Ford snorted, and Kari knew he'd been right to bring her with him. She responded for him. "Very. It was an *incredible* date. I enjoyed myself thoroughly. I'm sorry I stole Ford from you both this evening."

There was some hushed and frantic discussion she couldn't quite make out from Brady and Josh before she and Ford rounded the corner. Ford looked down at her and grinned.

She had never seen him this relaxed and happy— unguarded. It looked good on him. She promised herself then she'd do everything she could to put this expression on his face more often.

She squeezed his fingers as he led her deeper into his home. An expansive kitchen and dining area merged into an enormous lounge, complete with a grand piano and several modern chandeliers. The entire place sparkled and shone, even at night.

Brady and Josh were standing shoulder to shoulder near the couches. Brady finger-combed his hair before straightening a sexy pair of reading glasses she hadn't realized he used. Meanwhile, Josh smoothed his T-shirt over the lean muscles she remembered feeling beneath her hand as she braced herself against his torso during their kiss on the yacht. *Damn.*

She'd walked straight into a den. Instead of hungry bears or a pride of lions, there were three devastatingly attractive men waiting to pounce on her. Or her on them, if they weren't careful.

"Hey," Josh said with a bewildered smile. "I didn't expect to see you tonight."

"But of course we're thrilled you're here." Brady elbowed Josh, who nodded vigorously.

"Would you like a tour?" Ford asked her smoothly, covering for his partners.

"Absolutely!" She couldn't imagine there being more to the penthouse than this, which could easily fit four or five of her entire apartment inside it, but the gently curving staircase leading up to a second story above the high ceilings of the ground floor made her sure their private living quarters were just as grand as the main level.

"The best part of the place is the view," he said as he guided her past the gleaming grand piano and a humongous dining table that could easily seat a dozen people, to the wall of glass. "You'll have to come back to see it in the daytime."

She gulped, then nodded. Could this become somewhere she grew comfortable spending time? Would she ever fit in here? With them?

"Or better yet, stay over." Though Ford said it with a wink, Kari wasn't gullible enough to think he was entirely joking.

Scarier, she wasn't sure she wanted to turn down his pseudo-offer.

"There's a patio out there, too, with a pool and room for laying out or barbequing in the summer," he added when she didn't respond to his teasing.

"Damn." Kari thought she might, for the first time, truly have gotten a feel for how much more well off they were than her. The realization had her shrinking from Ford some. Why did they want her? What could she have to give them that was anything even close to this?

She slid her fingers from Ford's and wrung her hands in front of her. "It's absolutely stunning, guys. Gorgeous."

Her gaze slid along the skyline, which was visible even in the dark thanks to the lights dotting the stringers of the bridges and the flashing warnings to planes overhead on the peaks of the buildings.

They lived on top of the world. She...didn't.

"Not nearly as amazing as you," Ford whispered in her ear. "Are you okay? Was it a bad idea to bring you here?

We can go if you want. I'll take you home any time you're ready."

She shook her head no. As much as she didn't belong, she didn't want to leave yet either. "It's just that seeing your home makes it obvious how imbalanced things are between us. Any one of you guys is...everything. I'm nothing."

Kari shrugged, feeling like an imposter in her department store dress, which—while lovely—was nothing like the finery she'd worn the night of Ford's birthday party. The outfit they'd bought for her. If they took this further, they'd always be raising her to their level. And that didn't sit right. She wanted to earn her way to the top herself, not by fooling around with them.

"I never want to hear you say that again." Ford put his hands on her shoulders and shook her lightly. Not in a threatening way, but one that got her rapt attention. He said, "You're not nothing. You're everything. I admire your spirit, how resilient you are. How capable and kind. Generous with your time and empathetic. You're gorgeous, of course. And you always have your shit together. Somehow, you manage to keep us three in line, which isn't easy."

"You seriously think I have my shit together?" She leveled an incredulous gaze at him. His confident assertion rocked her to her core. How could he really believe that after he'd seen her earlier? "That's funny, because I constantly feel like I'm falling apart."

"Who doesn't?" Ford shrugged one shoulder. "Life is hard. Every day has its challenges and yours have held more than most lately. Yet you're here, surviving. I'm impressed by you every single day. We're lucky to have you in our lives. And that's not *nothing*."

Kari melted inside. He really believed what he was saying. They weren't empty compliments. She could read the conviction in his steely gaze. It was the same look he leveled at juries during passionate closing arguments. The one that nearly always resulted in a win for their firm and their clients.

"Wow." She cleared her throat. "Thank you. That means a lot coming from you."

Her words felt inadequate to express her gratitude. It had been so long since she'd felt confident in her abilities and her worth. With one date, he'd changed her perspective. Given her something far more valuable than even this ridiculous penthouse they now stood in.

Stood so close in...

While Josh and Brady watched on in utter silence, Kari leaned forward, breathing deep of the warm vanilla spice of Ford's aftershave and cologne. He was even more delicious than the dessert they'd shared at the restaurant earlier. He made her mouth water for a taste of him. Just a single nibble.

And she hoped she could stop there.

Knowing full well that Josh and Brady were paying close attention across the room, observing their every move even if they couldn't quite hear the subdued conversation, she beamed up at Ford. "I think you're pretty amazing yourself, you know. And tonight has been better than I could ever have dreamed."

"I'm glad you enjoyed it as much as I did." Ford put his hand against her cheek, his fingers in her hair, and swiped her cheek with the pad of his thumb.

"It's about to get better," she whispered, and then reached up to him.

Kari put her arms around his neck and tugged him until their mouths aligned.

"Are you sure?" he murmured, hovering there until she nodded nearly imperceptibly.

Then he groaned and lunged forward. He wasn't sweet like Josh had been. He was aggressive. His hands captured her face and led her where he could please them both most. It thrilled her to know he thought her capable of accepting his intensity. The bold sweep of his tongue, which parted her lips, made her feel strong. The electricity of their kiss flooded through her, making her crave more of this feeling. Whatever it took to get it.

After who knew how long, Kari had to come up for a breath. She rested her forehead on his shoulder, loving how tall and broad he was. Never once did she feel threatened, only sheltered.

It was then she realized the noise in the background was whistling and clapping from Brady and Josh. Brady's voice was huskier than usual when he called, "Damn! That looked amazing. I can't wait for my turn."

"Who says you have to wait?" Kari asked, then flicked her slightly unfocused stare up to Ford. "Do you mind?"

"Hell no. You don't have to ask for my permission either. You're in charge here," he promised.

Part of her wished she wasn't, but she figured they could discuss that some other time. When she wasn't focused on sampling each of them and evening the score. The worst possible outcome of this reckless, wanton behavior would be if she caused an imbalance than led to a rift between them.

Kari crossed the room, heading directly for Brady. It was a long walk, and she actually felt sexy as she strutted toward him in her heels. He made her feel even more so as his gaze ping-ponged between her and Ford. Brady asked him, "You're good with this?"

"Absolutely," Ford said. When she looked over her shoulder at him for one last confirmation, he was touching his mouth as if he could still feel the tingle there, like she could, after their kiss.

She figured the best she could do was give him, and Josh, a hell of a spectacle to enjoy while she learned what it would be like to make out with her third boss. Brady was suave where Ford was forceful and Josh was likeable. He was a consummate gentleman.

So it didn't surprise her when he waited for her to approach, then reached for her hands instead of dragging her into an embrace. They were so warm when they wrapped around hers, his thumbs rubbing lightly across the backs of her hands as he stared down into her eyes.

"Hi," she said simply.

"Hello." One side of his mouth crooked up into a sinful smile. She'd always wondered what he would be like if he let go for just one moment. And now she intended to find out.

"Kiss me?" Kari didn't know where she found the courage to beg. Once the words flew from her lips, she refused to recall them.

"I thought you'd never ask." He grinned then, for just a flash, before he descended. His mouth was softer than Ford's had been, his face perfectly smooth, even at this time of night. He caressed instead of invading like Ford had or cajoling like Josh had the night of the party.

Kari sighed and molded to him, her insides going molten. Each of the three men now surrounding her brought something unique to their partnership, and she could see how perfectly they would complement each other in bed, just like they did in the office.

What had started as an innocent enough exploration now seemed like kindling for a fire growing within her. Within them all if Brady's tightening clasp on her wrists, or Ford's low curse, or Josh's sigh of appreciation were any indication. She knew that once the blaze grew hot enough, there would only be one way to extinguish it.

A way that ended up with her and her bosses naked.

A way they could never come back from.

Right then, she didn't care. The rising sensations erased her inhibitions. She clasped Brady's head and drew him tighter to her. He did as she silently urged, deepening their kiss. He fluttered his tongue against hers, making her bones liquefy.

When she might have sagged against Brady or gone to the floor at his feet, Ford was there to support her. To hold her up and open for his best friend to devour. Not only did he approve of their connection, he encouraged it. Her wicked thoughts became his dirty talk.

"That's right, Kari. Take what you need. Show him how much you want him. It's not going to end with a kiss, is it? That could never be enough, am I right?"

"Yes!" Her cry was garbled against Brady's skilled mouth, but it was clear enough to the men sharing this moment with her.

They came closer, surrounding her.

## 16

---

"**Y**ou guys, hang on a second," Kari gasped, trying to catch her breath.

Immediately, they froze. Absolute faith blossomed inside her for the first time in months. They were gentleman, even if unconventional ones. They would never do something she wasn't completely onboard with. Even if she changed her mind at the last moment, they would respect and honor her decision.

That alone gave her such a rush, she had to have an outlet for all her joy and hope and a sexual urgency she had been afraid she might never experience again after what had happened at that fateful office party.

With Ford, Brady, and Josh, she was in six very capable hands—ones that would rather break themselves than mistreat her. Instead, they promised to deliver ecstasy like she'd never felt before.

"What's wrong?" Ford asked without a hint of frustration. He truly cared about her wellbeing.

"I don't think it's a good idea to go forward. I can't get over knowing we work together. I appreciate that you've been able to keep things separate. But I'm afraid that *I* can't. Once we do this, I don't know that, when we're at the office, I'll be able to pretend like it didn't happen or won't happen again." She bit her lip, looking out over the city to avoid their disappointment. Everything inside her screamed that she knew how to solve this problem. She only hoped that one night was enough to make up for what she was about to sacrifice.

"If you want me—or Bronson—to take you home, that's completely understandable," Ford offered.

"But if you'd like to stay, I hope you know that whatever happens here tonight has no bearing on your job or anything related to work. Uh...in either direction, better or worse." Josh shrugged one shoulder, drawing her attention back to him.

Dear God, could they think she'd use her performance in bed as a way to twist them for a raise or some shit? That did it. No. There was no way she could fool around with them while she was their executive assistant.

Kari cleared her throat, then made sure her voice was loud enough that all three of them heard her perfectly clearly. "You know what? I quit."

They didn't react like she'd expected. No persuasion or shock or outrage followed.

Josh grabbed his stomach and cracked up until he doubled over in his fit of laughter. Ford chuckled and Brady bumped his shoulder into Josh's. "Quit it, you're ruining the mood."

A tiny sliver of Kari's ego shriveled because they didn't seem to care about losing her at work. But then she told herself it was because they wanted this more. So did she, or she wouldn't have given up a job she loved and excelled at for a chance at something greater.

She could find another place to work. She couldn't replace the three men surrounding her right then. They were worth the risk.

"Then why don't you come over here and get us back on track?" she asked Brady.

"Seriously? You want...more?" He leaned in, staring into her eyes.

She nodded, sending her long hair tumbling around her. Compared to the tight buns she normally wore to the office, it must have made her look different, more feminine, to them. Because Ford licked his lips, Josh went quiet, and Brady flat-out reached for her.

Leaving the house earlier in the evening, she hadn't thought that her night might end like this, but she couldn't rein in the euphoria that Brady's touch caused. She sighed and leaned into his hand, which cupped her upper arm.

"How far do you want us to take this?"

"Can we see where it goes?" she wondered. "Or is that unfair? I don't want to leave you guys hanging if I reach my limit." Her logical side tried to assert itself, but reasoning was nearly beyond her as arousal began to drive her reactions.

"We're more than capable of taking care of ourselves," Ford told her. "Don't worry about us. We want tonight to be for you. We want to show you what we have to give. This is new for us, too. We've never been with someone who cares about us, like you do. That's all that matters."

Kari nodded. She couldn't say where she found the courage to be so bold, but she held her hand up and out to Ford. He took it and squeezed. When she tugged, he stepped nearer. "Sit behind me? Hold me?"

"Of course." He did as she directed, climbing onto the

enormous sofa and settling her against his chest. The position reminded her of her fantasy, which only excited her more. It also meant his hands were free to roam up and down her arms, and even across the tops of her breasts, which her dress left exposed.

She shivered.

"Where do you want me?" Josh asked, looking as eager to please her as a faithful puppy.

Kari stared right at him as she spread her legs as far as the skirt of her dress would allow. It was far enough to make room for him between them. She patted the sofa. "Here."

He shot her a wicked grin as he crawled toward them and sprawled between her legs, resting his head on her thigh. Naturally, her fingers went to his head, splaying in his soft blond hair.

"And me?" Brady wondered.

"I want to kiss you again. I didn't get enough before."

"I don't think I could ever get enough of you," Ford whispered into her ear. She loved when he did that, as if he was sharing a secret with her. Telling her how much she meant to him, although it was difficult for him to express himself so candidly. He usually kept his emotions under tight reins.

Kari's new goal was to shatter his control.

She thought she might just do it too when she leaned back, opening herself to Brady and Josh's approach while reaching down, snaking her hand between them, simultaneously. Her fingers brushed over Ford's hard-on, which had made itself obvious against the small of her back.

Damn, even if he had a dozen pairs of underwear on, padding that thing, he was bigger than the handful of guys she'd been with before. Her fingers reflexively closed around his bulge, making him curse and thrust into her touch.

Oh yeah, definitely bigger.

Kari looked over her shoulder and said, "Maybe you should get rid of your clothes. I think you're overdressed."

He groaned, then nodded. With some contortionist-worthy maneuvers, he shed his shirt and dress pants, leaving only his boxer briefs in place. The hairy muscles of his calves bracketed her, making her feel secure and cradled as Brady took in the view.

"Jealous?" she asked him.

"Not exactly. Envious, though? Yeah." He grimaced as he looked down the front of his pajama pants. "If I'd known you were coming over, I would have planned to sleep naked tonight."

"How is that different from any other night?" Josh asked from where he lounged between her legs, trailing his fingers down her exposed calf, making her squirm against Ford.

"Okay, it's not." Brady smiled.

"A man after my own heart," Kari teased. "Nothing better than sliding into fresh sheets without any clothes on."

Ford, Brady, and Josh went completely silent at that. Their coiled muscles and tight jaws made her realize just how turned on they were by that revelation. And how much they really wanted her.

She figured it was time she let go so they could show her what they were really capable of. "Look, can I be honest?"

Ford hugged her from behind. "Of course, you can tell us anything. We want you to share how you're feeling so we don't make any mistakes. This is important to us. Everything, remember?"

She nodded. "What I want most of all is to stop thinking. To lay back and feel. To do what comes naturally and fuck the rest. I'm so tired, guys. Tired of always worrying about the consequences of my actions and about the past. I want to live for tonight."

"We can help you with that," Brady promised.

"In fact, that sounds like Ford's specialty." Josh beamed at her and at the man behind her, cradling her against his strong body.

She tipped her head to the side so she could see his face when she asked, "It is?"

"Yeah. You may have noticed, I like to be in charge." His wry grin made her certain he didn't always like that side of himself. He might not, but she sure as hell did.

"Do it. Be the man you were meant to be. Show me who you really are. Please," she whispered before going slack in his hold, melting into him.

Ford growled before addressing Brady and Josh. "Tonight is all about her. Understand?"

"Fuck." Brady hissed as he shifted, his growing erection obvious in his thin pants.

"Do you hear what I'm saying?" Ford asked again, this time while staring at Josh.

"Yeah, I got it." Josh closed his eyes, then angled his head so he could press a kiss to her thigh. He breathed deep and she wondered if he could smell her arousal and what being around them like this did to her. She imagined the answer was yes when he looked up at her, his eyes darkening by the second.

"May we take your clothes off?" he asked.

Kari's eyes went wide. The thought of being on display

for them did funny things to her insides, but it made her uneasy, too. Being that vulnerable...being the *only* one that vulnerable...didn't sit right with her. "Only if I can see you, too."

Brady shrugged one shoulder and shucked his shirt before she could finish her thought. His abdomen was far more ripped than she had imagined many times, based on his trim frame. No wonder those dress shirts hugged him so damn well.

Josh did the same. Both men had a hand at their waistband, waiting for her assent, in seconds.

Kari nodded and it was done. Brady stepped out of his pants, gloriously naked before her. His body was worthy of being sculpted and hoarded in a museum for people to admire for centuries. She felt like she could easily spend that long learning every dip and curve of his form. With her hands...and her tongue.

Brady must have approved of her gawking. He stepped forward and kissed her, giving her what she'd asked for earlier. He took her breath away and when he paused, pulling away, all she could do was sigh.

That didn't take anything away from Josh, either. He was shorter and a little more muscular, though every bit as handsome. She reached for him, and he came. His mouth was on hers before she had to beg him to kiss her again, like he had the week before.

This time, though, she could feel the warmth of his skin directly on her palms. It felt amazing to caress him while he made out with her. Ford's cock firmed even more behind her, letting her know—as surely as his murmured praise did—how much he enjoyed watching her unravel in his arms, thanks to the efforts of one of his best friends.

It was only then that she realized he was toying with

the zipper at the back of her dress. He hesitated, as if afraid of triggering her again.

She paused her kiss with Josh, sucking on his bottom lip as they parted, then glanced over her shoulder. "Go ahead."

"Are you sure?" Ford wondered. "We can take this slower if you're not comfortable..."

"I'll be a hell of a lot more comfy once you get rid of this dress." She wriggled, causing the tight skirt to ride up her thighs even as she began to push the top lower. Her breasts threatened to spill from the sweetheart neckline.

Josh licked his lips as Brady sank down beside him.

"You're gorgeous, Kari," Ford told her before reclaiming her lips for himself. The combination of his fierce possession and Josh's playful kiss and Brady's seductive one had her writhing between his legs. As impressive as his cock felt behind her, its length laid along her spine, she was glad they didn't push her beyond this comfortable, safe zone they'd set up between them.

She wanted to do things with them that she hadn't with Marty. Things that hadn't been used against her.

Kari shook her head and reached blindly for Josh and Brady, ready to replace bad memories with good ones. Fortunately, Ford was thinking much more clearly than she was. He barked orders to his friends. "Brady, get rid of her dress. Josh, you keep her comfortable."

She wasn't sure exactly what he meant by that until Josh slipped her shoes from her feet and tossed the steep heels off to the side. He massaged her soles, making her whimper.

It was an incredible distraction from the cool air that washed over her as Brady peeled the bodice of her dress away from her chest. He nuzzled her breasts, laying soft kisses over the mounds of them before progressing lower. He walked the fabric down to her waist, then waited for Ford to wrap his hands around her waist and lift her off the couch just enough for him to finish sliding her dress off her.

The entire time, Josh was petting her, rubbing her legs and calves, soothing her as they arranged her open and waiting for their attention. When her flesh was bared to them, he traveled upward, his parted mouth washing her with his warm breath, which feathered over her sensitized skin.

And when he reached the edge of her skimpy lace panties, he breathed deep before skipping over them to press his face against her stomach while his hands kneaded endlessly at her hips and thighs.

Kari spread her legs wider, hoping for more contact. They were driving her wild, making her want things she shouldn't hope for. She didn't care. All she knew was what her body demanded.

Better yet, Ford knew, too. "Brady, get her bra next. Show me her tits."

A breath wheezed out of her, but rather than tensing, she went slack, relying on Ford's arms to hold her up even as his control kept their interaction in line with her desires.

"Yes," he whispered as he kissed her neck, making her shiver. "Let us take care of you. I swear we will. We won't let you down again."

Kari wanted to argue that they never had, but she couldn't find the words right then. Especially not when Brady whisked away her bra and replaced the fabric with his mouth. All she could do was hold on, her fingers clasping his head to hold him close to her chest as he suckled first one nipple and then the other until they were hard, aching peaks desperate for more stimulation.

Ford's hand snaked around her and squeezed the tip of one, enhancing the work his partner had done to get her ready for his firmer touch. She moaned and bucked, her hips shifting restlessly on the couch. She might have slid off it onto the floor if it hadn't been for Josh, who held her steady.

With Ford enjoying her breasts and flooding her with pleasure, Brady moved on to her panties. He coordinated with Josh to lift her as he slid them down her legs. Then there was nothing between them. Any of them.

Kari gulped, then reached for Brady's cock, which was hard and long and looked like it could use some attention. Ford made a guttural sound that Brady understood, even if she didn't. He sidestepped her touch and shook his head as he smiled down at her.

"Not tonight, Kari." He leaned down and kissed her until she forgot to object before murmuring, "Tonight is yours."

She gasped into his mouth as Ford cupped her breast fully in his palm and squeezed. Josh smothered her in kisses starting at her pubic bone, heading lower, lower.

When she pried her eyes open and peeked at him, she saw him looking up at Ford, who nodded. "Show her how good you are at eating pussy."

Kari might have made a fool out of herself with her gasp if Brady hadn't been there to devour it. He made love to her lips as Josh put his mouth between her legs and began to prove that Ford hadn't been exaggerating. Ford's other hand stroked down her ribs, then to her thigh. He cupped it and pulled, spreading her open for Josh to enjoy.

"Are you okay with this?" he whispered into her ear.

"Yes!" she shouted into Brady's mouth as her hips arched up, fusing her core tighter to Josh's skilled lips. He took the opportunity to extend his tongue and begin lapping her slit. By the time he had wrapped his mouth around her clit and began to suck, she knew she wasn't going to last long in their arms.

Simply being between them had her more turned on than full penetration with other people had in the past. Whether it was because it was so taboo to be the object of desire of three wickedly sexy men or because she cared so much for each of them, she wasn't sure. But she wasn't about to stop to think about it then.

Kari arched into Ford's hold.

"You like this, don't you?" he asked. "Are you going to come so soon? You're fucking amazing, Kari."

She wished she could make this feeling last forever, but her body wasn't going to be able to resist the promise they were making with their coordinated efforts.

Josh lifted his head long enough to say, "Ford, you've got to feel her. I can see her clenching. I bet she'd love your fingers inside her."

It was obvious he could have inserted his own digits within her if that's what he wanted. No, he needed his friend to do this with him. With them.

And Ford must have needed it, too.

Kari grasped his hand and dragged it toward her pussy. She stared into Brady's eyes as Ford pressed into her. She shuddered when he filled her, curling his finger to touch just the right spot to make her see stars.

"Fuck, you're so hot. And tight. And wet." He breathed just below her ear as he explored her from within. "I can't wait to feel you come on my hand, and Josh's face."

Well, that was a good thing. Because Kari couldn't resist such blatant desire or the way they amplified her arousal. She splayed her legs over Ford's thighs, arched her spine so her mound pressed as tight as possible to Josh's mouth and the wonderful things he was doing to her.

Then she deepened her kiss with Brady, feeding him every bit of her pleasure. He groaned, his eyes desperate on hers.

Ford rumbled, his voice huskier than before. "Brady, slide your hand under my leg. I bet you can work a finger in her too."

When the blunt tip pressed against her opening, Kari shuddered, on the verge of losing control. Her mind blanked and all she could do was revel in the euphoria they were inducing. It was exactly what she'd asked for. They were everything she'd needed, even if she didn't understand exactly what that was before.

She held Ford and Brady within her while Josh toyed with her clit.

When he licked lower and wriggled his tongue against her opening, pressing the slightest bit inside between his partners' fingers while his nose nudged her clit, she lost all semblance of control.

Kari stretched tight, her back bowed, her head resting on Ford's shoulder. She sucked on Brady's tongue while Ford's hand clasped her breast and his other began to slide in and out of her. Josh increased the pressure of his tongue and face, buried in her pussy, until she shattered.

She flew apart as she came on them, pressing them together within her until she thought they might fuse into a single tool that brought her more pleasure than she could have dreamed was possible. Her orgasm went on and on. It wrung her dry, left her exhausted and so sated that she couldn't have moved if she wanted to.

That didn't stop the guys from taking care of her, though. They withdrew from her body and began to tend to her. Cleaning her up and arranging her between them on the oversized sectional. She hummed, floating in a daze of rapture.

Ford stroked her hair, Brady told her over and over how amazing she was, and Josh stared at her with pure awe and admiration in his gaze. It was one of the few times she'd seen him this serious.

"That was..." She huffed. "Wow."

They deserved something more eloquent than that simple declaration. Except they'd wrecked her. Utterly destroyed her capacity to do anything other than bask in the gift they'd given her. And before she realized what they were doing, they were redressing her as if to ensure they didn't break their own rules and take things further than they'd already gone.

Once she was safely zipped into her dress once more, Ford kissed her shoulder. "You're everything we've been looking for. Thank you so much for trusting us. I can't wait to see where we go from here."

Kari nodded. He was right. She had to think about that, too.

Now that she'd taken this step toward them and away from the life she'd had before, she had a lot to figure out. And quick. She asked quietly, "Would you mind having Bronson give me that ride home now?"

Though Josh turned his face, it wasn't fast enough for her to see the flash of hurt and disappointment there. If she didn't get this right, she would ruin things before they're gotten started.

To do that, she needed some space to think. And plan.

She reached out and hugged Josh before promising, "I don't regret this. I just need some time to adjust to how much our lives are about to change, okay?"

"Of course," Brady answered for him. "Just so you know, though...our lives haven't been the same since we met you."

Ford nodded his agreement, then rose, offering his hand to help her from the couch. Her legs shook but held as she strode, spine straight and head high, toward her purse while Josh called Bronson and asked him to take Kari home and see her safely inside.

She felt stronger than ever knowing how deeply they desired her and what they were willing to do to have a shot at making this last for the long run. Kari couldn't be any less brave and still deserve all the promises they'd made her that night, so she kissed them each goodnight, then left to get her world in order.

## 17

Ford sat at his desk and checked his watch. Again. "Brady, still no word from Kari?"

"Not yet," he called from his office next door. The sound of his executive chair scooting was followed by him, and then Josh a few steps behind, tromping through Ford's office doorway. "What the fuck is going on?"

"Guys. She's only twenty minutes late." Josh held his hands out, but this time he said it with a hell of a lot less conviction than he'd said, "Guys, she's only five minutes late," fifteen minutes before.

Brady rubbed his temple. "She's worked here for five years and never once gotten here after us. Never. Never called in sick either. And today..."

"It can't be a coincidence." Dread settled in the pit of Ford's gut. He knew he was right. "I don't think she was joking last night."

"About what?" Josh asked.

"Quitting. She's not coming back. Today or any other day." Ford rose from his chair and punted his aluminum trashcan into the wall. "Fuck!"

While the night before had been one of the best of his life, he hadn't realized it meant sacrificing seeing Kari all day, every day. Not to mention her surrendering her job. One she was incredible at.

"The last thing I wanted was for us to cost her anything." Brady put his face in his hands. "I was thinking more emotionally, not wanting to freak her out or bring back bad memories. But this...if she's unemployed because of us..."

Josh groaned. "She's going to resent us for this."

"I wouldn't blame her if she did." Ford pounded his thigh with his fist. "Maybe it's not too late to fix this. Brady, can you call her? You're the best at talking shit out. Make her understand that we need her here as much as at home. And if that means she doesn't want to see us again after hours..."

The three men exchanged pained looks. Josh nodded and Brady grimaced before sighing. "Yeah. Okay. You're right."

He drew his phone from the pocket of his meticulously tailored suit pants, then tapped the only speed dial icon on his home screen. Ford held his breath as Brady swallowed hard. Hopefully he was thinking about what to say when Kari picked up.

Except she didn't.

The sweet sound of her voice requesting that he leave a message was barely audible from where he stood across his desk from Brady. Damn it! "Try again."

Brady hung up and redialed. With the same results. Except this time her greeting floated from the speaker after just two rings. She was sending them straight to voicemail. Son of a bitch!

"Uh oh." Brady frowned at the phone in his hand.

They hadn't devised a plan by the time her voicemail beeped, letting them know it was recording. So he improvised, "Kari, it's us. We're waiting for you at the office. Please let us know you're okay and when you'll be here. Thanks. I know it's only been a few hours but...I miss you. *We* miss you."

Ford reached across the space between them and disconnected the line. "You can't do that! Don't blackmail her with feelings. She told us she couldn't fuck her bosses and we told her we're not going to force her to do anything she doesn't want to do. I should have taken her seriously last night."

"Oh shit." Josh sank into one of the guest chairs in front of Ford's desk. "What did we do?"

"Don't freak out yet. First, we need to find her and make sure she's okay. If she regrets her decision, we have to give her job back and promise to keep our fucking hands off her from now on." Ford stared at Brady and Josh.

Brady shook his head. "I don't know if I can. Maybe *I'll* be the next one to quit."

This time Ford knew his friend wasn't kidding.

What they'd done, though it had only seemed like dipping a toe in the pool of their desires, might already have led them to disaster. Ford didn't want to lose any of them, Kari or the guys. They'd built this place together and they all deserved to enjoy their success while helping it grow.

It wasn't often he felt helpless.

None of them got much work done as they waited to hear from Kari. The hours that passed without her returning their calls seemed to stretch for a month. If it was this bad after a single evening spent in her company, what would happen if they got in deeper and then lost her entirely?

Ford realized then how high the stakes were in this game they'd been playing.

Did that mean they should take things slower or get a hell of a lot more serious?

## 18

K ari beamed as she reached across the table and shook her new boss's hand. The CEO's wolfish grin made her sure he considered himself just as lucky to have her on board, ready to organize and streamline the shit out of his company.

The morning hadn't gone anything like she'd imagined. It was crazy to think that just a few hours ago, she'd called Andi hoping for a sounding board and had instead ended up with a new job. Just like that.

One with a raise, even.

And extra responsibilities.

Well, damn. Maybe last night hadn't been the biggest mistake of her life after all.

Of course, her position as the office manager of the scientific research and development firm Andi worked for didn't have the intangible benefit of three sexy bosses to drool over all day. However, it did allow her to work in a place uncomplicated by her personal desires.

After the night before, she was sure she could never look at Ford, Brady, or Josh impersonally again. The

things they'd done to her...the way they'd made her feel...
No, not possible to forget that.

She couldn't wait to share her news with them and, hopefully, spend tonight celebrating this next step toward a healthy relationship with them.

"You just have to promise me one thing," her new boss said as he walked her to the door.

"What's that?" She hesitated. Could there be a catch?

"When the lawyers over at Westbrook, Arman, and King try to sue me for stealing you away from them, you have to protect me."

Kari cracked up. "That's not going to be a problem. They've probably already replaced me."

That thought caused a lump in her throat that she wasn't able to clear easily. Her smile wilted some imagining some other person taking care of her guys' business.

"I'd be willing to bet my corner office that's not the case. But their loss is my gain." The CEO chuckled as he walked her to the door. "I'll see you tomorrow for your first official day, okay?"

"I can't wait." She pivoted on her heel, trying not to do a little boogie on her way out.

Kari made it to the lobby of the building before fishing in her purse for her cellphone. When she unlocked it and swiped her finger over the settings to turn the ringer back on, she saw she had seven missed calls. All from Ford, Brady, and even a couple from Josh.

Oops.

She pasted a smile on her face when just moments before she hadn't had to try. Glee had poured out of her. Now, nervous electricity zinged through her like it had before her stellar interview. What did they need to say to her?

Were they calling to tell her to come back to work because last night had been enough?

They better not be.

Now that she'd had one taste, she needed more. A lot more.

Not only of the mind-blowing sex they'd introduced her to the night before, but also the fun they'd had. The laughter and easy familiarity they'd shared ranked right up there with the tender, intimate moments, and the lust-fueled ones, too. She'd be lying if she didn't admit it had a lot to do with security as well. Ford had made her feel safe. Even in that awkward moment when she'd let her imagination run wild and the darkness inside her had threatened to ruin everything.

After climbing into a taxi, Kari allowed herself to stop speculating about what they wanted and find out. She pressed play on the first voicemail recording. She'd received it at 8:05. "Hey, Kari, it's Ford. I just wanted to check and make sure you're okay since you're never late. Anyway, let us know if something's up. Otherwise, I'll see you soon."

Professional. But still with an underlying hint of worry. *Uh oh.*

Kari thought back to when she'd tendered her resignation. They'd laughed.

Oh fuck. It wasn't because they didn't care or because they saw it as some kind of a victory to have her at home instead of at work. They hadn't taken her seriously.

She drooped forward, her forehead *thunking* onto the seatback in front of her.

Sure enough, one after the other, the guys' calls had

grown more urgent. Most of all she felt bad that she'd stressed them. Somewhere around the fifth voicemail, this one from Brady, she realized they'd figured it out.

"Hey, Kari. I think you're really not coming in anymore. That's...okay. I understand. But could you please just call so we know you're all right with...everything? Thank you." He sounded so defeated. Not at all his usual, confident self.

Even after facing a loss in the courtroom, he never sounded like that.

Desolate.

For the first time, Kari understood that she had the power to hurt the guys, too. Maybe even more than they could do to her. The revelation shocked her. And made her certain that this morning's meeting had been exactly the way to go.

Things were complicated enough between them. This would help. It balanced the power. It made her feel more confident about being a true partner to them and less concerned about the ramifications a falling out could have on her career. She was free now to explore with them.

And that was worth the sacrifice.

Now she just had to convince the guys of that.

## 19

Brady looked up from the mountain of papers on his desk when movement in his peripheral vision made him aware of someone approaching. "Kari! You're here!"

He dropped the investigator's report he'd been scrutinizing and flew around his desk toward her. When she held up her hand, palm out—in the classic signal for stop—he froze. "Can you come into Ford's office for a second? I want to talk to the three of you together."

Well, that didn't sound good.

Kari turned and hustled out of the room toward Josh's office. He heard his friend's equally optimistic greeting before they piled into Ford's space, somber as they waited to hear their fate from her lush lips.

Ford stood. "You're okay?"

Kari nodded. "I'm fine. Sorry I worried you."

Brady closed the door quietly behind them, then shuffled as close as he dared. He didn't want to invade her personal space, though part of him needed so badly to be near her. To make sure they hadn't damaged the budding relationship he thought they were nurturing the night before.

Ford was right. They had to be more careful from now on. Take things slower.

"I feel like an asshole for laughing at you last night," Josh said then, drawing her attention to him. "I thought you were joking about quitting. You know it's not necessary for you to be unemployed because of what happened."

"I'm not." She shrugged.

"So you're coming back then?" Brady put his hands on his knees and drew a shaky breath. Oh thank God.

"No." She shook her head with a wince. "I got a job this morning. I start tomorrow as the office manager over at Blackstone Industries."

"You what?" Ford asked.

"Damn, Kari..." Josh whistled. "That didn't take long."

"Hold up. Isn't that where Andi works?" Brady tipped his head.

She nodded. "But I got the job on my own merits. Andi knew of the opening and put in a call to HR for me. The rest was all me."

Brady held up his hands. "Hey, you don't think I know that? They're lucky to have you. Losing you is an enormous blow to this firm."

"And to us," Josh muttered.

Ford stayed quiet, which troubled Brady the most. He stared at his friend, praying the other man didn't explode and ruin their chances with Kari. If they couldn't have her during the day, maybe that meant she was ready to give them her nights.

He would take what he could get. "Well, since you

don't work here anymore...does that mean I can take you out for a few celebratory drinks tonight?"

Kari smiled. It started out slow then spread across her face, making her even more beautiful than he had already known she was. Her eyes shone a little when she said, "I would love that. Thank you."

Josh high-fived Brady. Then he turned to Kari, clearly wanting to get in on the action himself. "How about Friday we go see that movie you've been talking about?"

This time she sniffled. Had she been afraid they would change their minds?

She bit her lip, then nodded.

Ford approached her slowly. He stopped a few feet away and held out his arms to Kari. She raced into them. He enfolded her, then whispered against her hair, "Congratulations. I'm proud of you for going after what you deserve and doing what you think is right. We'll always stand by your decisions."

"And be the happiest guys in the world when you succeed like we know you will." Brady stepped closer. Kari squirmed until Ford reluctantly let her go. She took turns hugging and then kissing each of them.

Ford pulled away before things could get too steamy. Brady was both disappointed and grateful that his partner had enough self-control for them all. After this morning, and the terrifying thought of scaring Kari away, none of them wanted to make that mistake again.

"Have a good time with Brady tonight. Then maybe tomorrow night we can have a congratulations dinner at our house together," Ford suggested.

"That would be amazing. But only..." Kari hesitated.

They would give her anything she asked for if only she'd keep giving them a chance to prove what Brady already knew to be true: this was something special. Something worth fighting for.

"What?" he wondered.

"You have to let me cook for you guys. Ever since those charred brownies you brought in to share, I don't trust you guys in the kitchen."

"That was Josh's fault." Ford shook his head. "He set the timer for fifteen hours instead of fifteen minutes. We rescued them when the smoke alarm went off, but..."

"It was too late. They were dead." Kari laughed. "I might not be Julia Child, but I can make something you'll enjoy, I'm sure."

"I think after a couple days apart, I'm mostly going to be hungry for time with you," Ford said. It was what they were all thinking.

"I'm going to miss you, too." Kari sighed as she stared out at the city beyond them for a moment before shaking it off. "It will make me that much more excited to see you every night. Right?"

Kari probably hadn't meant that exactly like it sounded. Neither did she take it back when Ford hummed, Brady licked his lips, and Josh cracked his knuckles. It seemed like they were all ready to take this next step forward together.

"I'll pick you up at six. Sound good?" Brady asked.

Kari smiled. "No. It sounds perfect."

## 20

"How's it going so far, Kari?" Andi asked her at what was becoming their traditional lunch date in the company's cafeteria.

"Honestly, the work is fine. It's pretty easy." She shrugged one shoulder.

"I heard you have the entire department running ten times more efficiently already." Andi snorted. "That's pretty damn impressive. I mean, us scientists aren't the easiest to wrangle."

"They've got nothing on lawyers," Kari admitted with a wry smile.

"Do you miss working with your guys or is it a relief?" Andi wondered.

"Both, especially now. I want to spend more time with them rather than less. Like pretty much every minute of every day. But I know it's not good for my mental health, or whatever the hell this is growing between us, for me to be so wrapped up with them either. Or for me to be worrying about my job every time we hook up or if we fight, not that we have...yet." Kari thought some tension

149

was building, though mostly because they hadn't revisited the physical intimacy of the night of her first date with Ford since then.

"Maybe you need to be *more* wrapped up in them. That solves a lot of problems for me and my guys." Andi wiggled her eyebrows.

"Could be." Kari sure as hell could use an outlet to blow off some steam.

Since the night she'd quit, they'd spent every single evening getting to know each other better outside of work, yet the guys hadn't offered a repeat performance of their steamy session together. Neither had they pressured her for sex—individually or together.

The chaste pecks they gave her each night before Bronson drove her home were starting to make her batty. Did they think she couldn't handle what they'd done together because she'd pulled away professionally? She craved their heat and the exhilaration she'd felt when she was trapped between them. Didn't they?

"But ever since I quit, the guys have been different with me. Cooler. Pretty hands off, if you know what I mean."

"Maybe they're just worried they pushed you too hard, too fast." Andi put her sandwich down. "They're afraid of losing you entirely."

"Did they say that to you?" Kari asked.

"Not in so many words. But when I stopped by their office to pick Cooper up two nights ago they asked me a shit ton of questions about how things got started with me and my guys. They wanted to know about how it made me feel to go from being roommates to lovers, if I was ever overwhelmed, what things freaked me out, how my assault at Flesh impacted my ability to be intimate, stuff like that. Damn, they are intense. I wouldn't want to be a witness in one of their cases."

Kari laughed. Yep, that sounded like Ford, Brady, and Josh. Ford especially. "Sorry they grilled you."

Although she felt bad for her friend, it did something to her insides to know that they were so concerned for her and trying their best to do things right. They were everything she'd ever hoped to find in a guy. She might have had high standards if it took three men to fulfill her entire wish list but, hey, she was fine with that.

With a wave of her hand, Andi dismissed Kari's concern. "I'm happy to help. I'm rooting for the four of you. You make a good team and I can tell you're all pretty serious about this. Otherwise you would have fucked, got it out of your system, and moved on to a simpler, easier relationship. This is hard. You're just starting. Don't feel bad if it takes a while to figure everything out between you. Hell, I left my guys before we got it right. I think it's sweet that they're trying to avoid a disaster like the one that caused me to walk away."

Kari pushed the broken bits of chips left on her plate into a mound with one finger. "So what do you think I should do if I want to move things forward between us?"

"If you're ready for more, say so directly. Ask for what you need. Communication is critical in any relationship, but especially one like ours." Andi shrugged. "I'm pretty sure they're more than willing. They're just waiting for a clear sign from you."

"You think so?" Kari grinned.

"Ummmm, yeah." Andi rolled her eyes. "I saw the way they were drooling over you at Ford's birthday party. I know they wish it was you they'd had down below that night instead of...well, you know."

"I'm pretty sure none of them regret seeing what you had to show them." Kari squashed the fizzle of jealousy that bubbled up then. They hadn't touched Andi. And her friend might be right. They might have been imagining themselves doing those things to her.

She hummed.

"So now it's your turn." Andi pointed with a french fry at Kari. "Girl, what kind of sexy undies do you have? Now would be the time to dust off that pair you bought on a whim but were never brave enough to actually wear before. You know, we all have those. Or at least I used to. Several have been destroyed in the making of a good time."

Kari tried not to blush. "I got rid of everything like that after..."

"Ah, shit. Marty? That fucker." Andi wiped her hand on her napkin as if the thought killed her appetite, too. Then she reached for her phone and rounded the table to perch on the booth seat next to Kari. "Let's see what they have at the boutique across the street. You know, they offer free delivery downtown."

"They do?" Kari leaned closed to Andi so she could see what the woman was bringing up on the screen.

"Hell yes. And you would look stunning in this." She poked a picture of a red satin thing that had more straps and lace than actual fabric holding it together.

"Oh. I don't know about that." Kari winced. It was smoking hot, but she wasn't exactly a model. "I've eaten a lot more chips than that woman has in her lifetime."

"Shut your face." Andi tapped a couple more buttons. "You're a, what...size twelve?"

Kari nodded.

"It's in stock and even on sale." Andi did a fist pump.

"It's a sign from the universe. In fact...consider it my contribution to the cause."

"What are you doing?" Kari lunged for Andi's phone, but it was too late. Her friend apparently shopped there enough that she had a one-click buy account. And it was done. Andi had ordered the outrageous lingerie for an afternoon delivery to their office.

"Don't worry. They bring it in a plain black bag. No one will know what's in there." Andi slung one arm around Kari's shoulder. "You can thank me on Monday. I have a feeling your weekend is going to make for some good lunch conversation."

It seemed only fair not to spare the juicy details since Ford, Brady, and Josh had gotten a first-hand look at Andi's relationship with her three men. And to be honest, it helped a ton to have someone who could understand to discuss this stuff with. Kari felt for the first time like things were falling into place.

Her past wasn't haunting her like it had.

She'd found three incredible men to protect and cherish her.

And now she wanted to give them all of herself. The parts she'd been suppressing for months. She was ready to set their sheets on fire and see where their newfound freedom could take them if they weren't holding back.

Kari's life had somehow transformed itself, nearly overnight. She had friends, three incredible love interests, and a shot at the life she had only dreamed of before. These people understood her, knew about her past, and didn't give a fuck. They encouraged her to do what would make her the happiest even when it was scary.

And if she failed, at least she wouldn't have to work through it alone.

"Thank you, Andi." Kari hugged the other woman.

"You're welcome." Andi smiled at her. "You deserve this. You deserve them. Don't ever let yourself believe otherwise again."

Kari wiped moisture from the corner of her eye, refusing to cave to the urge to weep when everything in her life was perfect, amazing, and bursting with endless potential.

## 21

Kari picked up her ringing phone. She'd technically finished her shift fifteen minutes earlier and had been milling around tidying things up while she waited for the guys to let her know they were on the way for their usual evening pickup. She loved the time they spent together and the discussions they had during the trips to the penthouse—a place that was starting to feel like home to her, too.

What would they think of the contents of the black bag tucked discreetly under her coat on her office chair? The sooner they came and got her, the sooner she would find out. The suspense was killing her.

She answered the call from Brady with a giant smile on her face. "There you are. Running late, I assume?"

It was kind of a miracle that the guys had been on time to collect her from work every other day that week. She knew they didn't have typical jobs with a standard workweek. So she tried not to be too disappointed. Maybe tonight she'd have to go home to her empty apartment like she had before she'd officially started dating the guys.

Brady sighed. "I'm so sorry. I lost track of time. There was a significant development in the Peterson case today."

Kari twisted the handle of her bag around her finger before letting it unravel. "Hey, you sound like you're freaking out." Twist. Unravel. "I hope you're not planning on leaving that just to come and get me. If you give me an hour or so to go home and change, I'll even bring you guys some dinner down at the office. The three of you are working on it together, right?"

"Yeah. We'll probably be here all night. I'm sorry about that." At least he sounded as bummed as she felt about missing out on an evening spent together.

"I understand. This has always been your life. I don't expect you to change it for me." She truly didn't. Some part of her cheered that she could be useful to them. Take care of them again as she had for years now. And this time she wouldn't have to hide her deeper feelings. "You focus on what you have to do, and I'll be there soon with supplies to keep you guys fueled up for however long it takes. Okay?"

"Yeah, perfect. Thanks, Kari. You're a life saver."

"No problem." In fact...if she took some time to prepare herself properly, put on some makeup and the scraps of lace and silk in the bag beneath her coat, maybe she could help them de-stress some before going back to the grind.

More than once, especially lately, she'd imagined using that boardroom table for something a hell of a lot more fun than boring meetings. Somehow, she was sure Ford, at least, would be willing to indulge her fantasy.

Caught up in her wicked thoughts, she must have hesitated too long. Of course Brady noticed. "You sure you're okay? Maybe Andi wouldn't mind dropping you off instead," he suggested.

"She left about an hour ago. But it's no problem. I heard the weather is amazing this afternoon. A walk sounds great. Unless you need food sooner than…"

He dismissed her concerns. "No. Go ahead. Enjoy yourself. Swing by whenever you feel like it."

"I always feel like seeing you three." It kind of shocked her how much that first glimpse after being separated all day impacted her, making her heart stutter and her hands sweat.

Maybe it did the same to Brady, because he said, "Just say the word and I'll send Bronson to pick you up and bring you here right now or take you wherever you want to go first."

Kari laughed. "Don't be ridiculous. I'm hanging up now. I'll see you soon. I assume your usuals from Fugu are okay?"

"Yes. That sounds fucking amazing." Hell, they probably hadn't eaten all day if they were wrapped up in whatever it was that had their attention.

Kari didn't get a chance to ask because she heard Josh teasing Brady. "What's taking so long? Are you telling her we're slaving away at the office or having phone sex with her? Because if it's the latter, you better put her on speakerphone."

Was that an option? If she weren't in her workplace, Kari might have tested the waters.

"You're such an asshole, Josh. No, I'm begging her to bring us dinner. But for that, I'll eat your sushi, too," Brady huffed.

"Kari?" Josh hummed. "Sushi? How long do we have to wait?"

Kari wasn't sure if he sounded more excited about delivery or seeing her, but he sure did seem eager for her to arrive.

"Give me that hour, okay? I promise it will be worth it." She figured it would be close, but she could make it a little faster than that if she hustled. Assuming she could figure out where to put all those straps on the lingerie Andi had procured for her. Twist. Unravel.

"I like the way that sounds," Brady said. "We'll see you soon. Thanks again. And I promise we'll make it up to you this weekend, if you let us."

Kari shivered. She liked the sound of that. "Deal. Now let me go so I can get there quicker."

Brady made a noise that sounded like a kiss. He disconnected, but not before she heard Ford and Josh giving him shit for it.

Kari dropped her phone into her purse, tidied up her desk one last time, then headed out of the company's headquarters. She tipped her face up toward the setting sun and soaked in the rays. The orange and pink hues chasing each other across the sky had her in awe of nature and life and all the amazing things in it.

Including her three men. And bringing them some much-needed food. She missed looking after them. Which was exactly why she had to keep refusing their offers of raises and extra time off and whatever else they tried to use to bribe her into returning to their firm.

She wanted to lose herself in them so badly that she knew she couldn't allow herself to go all in like that. If things didn't work out...she'd be crushed. And have lost everything at once. No, keeping her professional life separate made her secure enough to take more risks on the personal front.

And this was personal.

So very personal.

Kari swung her purse as she strolled along, grinning like a crazy woman at the thought of her blossoming relationship with Ford, Brady, and Josh. They were everything she'd ever wanted and never imagined she'd find in a single guy. Well, because they weren't a single guy, she supposed.

Ford was responsible, a protector. Brady was romantic and sweet. Josh, fun and daring.

Together, they were perfect. Balanced. Complete.

Tonight was her chance to be what they needed. To nourish them, to replenish their energy so they could keep working through the night. Maybe she could give them massages or think of another way to relieve some of their tension.

Lost in her daydreams about what they might get up to later, she wasn't paying close attention to the smattering of people crisscrossing the sidewalk and streets surrounding her. She sidestepped to avoid a young man who stopped to talk into his action cam, probably vlogging about his day in their gorgeous city.

Most everyone in the business district had already headed home, but there were still enough people around that at first it didn't seem unusual that the footsteps behind her were so close and yet so perfectly in sync with hers.

Until she heard it. "Kari."

Ice immediately replaced the warmth of the sunset on her skin and the glow of her blossoming love—yes, she thought it—for Ford, Brady, and Josh in her heart.

She knew that voice.

It was him.

*Marty.*

But was it real or just another phantom of her wounded mind, like it had been when she'd imagined his face through the window at dinner with Ford?

Kari refused to let her dark past black out her bright future.

She straightened her spine and strode toward the crosswalk that would lead her to the safety of her apartment. Locked inside, she'd be able to shake this ominous sensation and the anxiety that was probably caused by knowing she was about to get a hell of a lot more intimate with the special men in her life.

"Hey! Don't ignore me. What? Are you too good for me now?"

That time she was sure the snarled command wasn't a figment of her twisted imagination.

Kari whipped around, putting herself off balance as she reached the curb. Traffic whizzed by, oblivious to the panic that exploded inside her. She glanced over her shoulder. A steady stream of cars flew at her back. Marty planted himself directly in front of her.

There was nowhere to run.

She should have screamed. Except when she opened her mouth, no sound would come out of her constricted throat.

Marty looked like he hadn't bathed since he'd been fired. His eyes were wild and his too-long, greasy hair flopped into them as he lunged toward her. "Was it fucking me that turned you on to lawyers?"

There was so much to object to in his statement that she couldn't decide which thing to refute first. Instead, he rambled on.

"I always knew you were asking for it. If I'd known the

problem was that you wanted more than one guy, I'd have brought some friends to the party." He sniffed, then swiped his hand over his nose. Was he on drugs?

As if sober Marty hadn't been bad enough. This was terrifying.

Kari took a step back and another, but quickly ran out of sidewalk.

"What's a matter? Don't act like you're not into it. I've seen you with them. Come with me and I'll take care of you right now. Otherwise..." He sniffed again, then grabbed for her arm.

Instinctively, Kari jerked to avoid contact with him.

No way was he ever going to touch her again.

Her foot repositioned to keep her steady. Instead of cement, it found only air when she put it back down.

Then she was falling. Stumbling, really, trying to stay upright by propelling herself into the street. With absolutely no other option, she flung her hand out toward Marty.

"Too late, bitch." Instead of grabbing it and hauling her to safety, he jammed his own arm toward her. His palm was flat where it connected with her sternum. Pressure from his shove propelled her farther into the street.

Her bags went flying. And so did she.

Marty kept walking as if nothing had happened.

The blare of a horn was the last thing she heard. Pain radiated from her hip as she crashed onto the hood of a car and tumbled.

The world went crazy. People screamed.

Moments stretched into an eternity.

Someone was asking if she was okay. She might have laughed at that if she could.

As her eyelids slammed shut against the riot of colors, sounds, and hurt, she imagined Ford, Brady, and Josh as they'd looked the night they'd given her so much pleasure. She hugged the memory tight to ward off her horror and agony.

Reality slipped away.

Dreams of happily ever after evaporated as nightmares descended.

———

KARI, Ford, Brady, and Josh's story concludes in book two of the Ever After Duet, *Fourkeeps*, available here.

**4-EVER THEIRS**
**JAYNE RYLON**
*NEW YORK TIMES BESTSELLING AUTHOR*

If you missed out on the 4-Ever series, start with 4-Ever Theirs to find out how Andi hooked up with her three roommates in the first place.

*One woman. Three dudes. No regrets.*

College was supposed to be Andi Miller's training ground for the real world. Instead, it's her final Saturday night in her college-grade apartment, and she's still sheltered as hell. Why? Because of her three adorable roommates—Reed, Cooper and Simon.

Determined to have one date where the overprotective trio doesn't scare the guy off, Andi sneaks out for the night. And almost lives to regret it.

When Reed, Cooper and Simon rescue Andi from a bad situation in the basement of a sex club, they decide it's time for the kid gloves to come off. Since their early college days, they've been not-so-secretly fighting amongst themselves to spark her next smile, her next laugh.

They've already done a lot of surviving together, and now it's time to thrive. At the risk of ruining a beautiful friendship, the men set out to turn their hands-off live-in arrangement into a weeklong learning experience where they become Andi's sex education teachers.

Except none of them realize their new found intimacy will make it impossible to say goodbye on graduation day.

**An Excerpt From 4-Ever Theirs:**

"Stop. Stop. I'm going to pee my pants." Andi Miller gasped between bouts of hysterical laughter. She swiped tears from her cheeks as her three obnoxiously adorable roommates demonstrated their best attempts at twerking from various places around their kitchen.

Sadly, Simon could definitely shake his ass better than she could. He put on quite a show from his perch atop their rickety table, threatening to turn it into kindling with sharp swings of his hips. The guy could easily have paid his portion of the rent and then some if he'd gotten a job as a go-go dancer.

"We're only trying to help." Cooper punched Simon in the leg then grappled him to the floor. If she didn't act fast, this could deteriorate into another of their infamous wrestling matches. The last one of those had resulted in the annihilation of a beanbag chair. She was still discovering tiny foam beads scattered throughout their apartment months later.

"I mean, it's not like you've come out of your room long enough to pick up any of our moves in the past four years, with all that studying you insisted on doing. You don't want to get embarrassed on the floor tonight, do you?" Reed asked as he simulated humping a cabinet.

Well, that wouldn't be a problem, seeing as she hadn't quite told them the truth about her destination for the evening. Dance club, hook-up spot—same difference, right?

Their over-protectiveness made her white lie necessary.

Besides, she owed them the same courtesy they showed her when it came to keeping their sex lives separate from their home lives.

The guys never brought women to the apartment. Or at least they hadn't in ages. Not since early in the first semester of their freshman year when one of their one-night stands—to this day, they wouldn't tell her which of them had slept with the poor girl—had tried to make herself some morning-after breakfast and ended up with a black eye courtesy of Andi's fist.

Hey, how was she supposed to have known it wasn't an intruder out there whipping up a frittata before absconding into the night with their meager college-grade possessions? Milk crate furniture might be hot on the black market for all Andi knew. If some of the oomph propelling her swing had actually been fueled by jealousy instead of fear, she'd hidden that pathetic fact as best she could from both herself and her roommates.

Ruining their friendships wasn't on her agenda. She wasn't the sort of girl who knew how to screw around then act like sex had been no big deal. Though she had chemistry with each of her roommates, how awkward would it have been to have followed through on it and slept with one of them?

Takeout and movie nights with the others would never have been the same.

Andi admitted it. She was sheltered as fuck. Though her vocabulary had gotten a hell of a lot more colorful as a result of her co-habbing with this trio of idiots for the past four years, she hadn't done a lot of exploring relationship-wise. After all, she spent most of her free time with

Cooper, Reed and Simon. Who would approach her with those three hovering over her, snarling and baring their teeth at any guy who got too close?

God, she was going to miss them.

The thought of giving up their second-to-last Saturday night together had her rethinking her plans. Except this might be her last chance to eliminate her regrets about not having a single fling during her college experience. It would help round out her academic studies and the rewarding social experiment living with three dudes had turned out to be.

This was supposed to be her training ground for the real world.

Now that she'd accomplished the majority of her goals —by graduating at the top of her class and scoring a prime position in her field—maybe she could make some time to fill the emptiness growing inside her as she accepted that she'd be forging out on her own soon. The lack of a relationship hadn't bothered her so much when she'd had school and her roommates' friendship to occupy her.

All of that was changing.

So was she.

Andi wanted to be ready for what came next.

"Was it that good for you?" Simon flashed a wicked smile as he teased her.

"Huh?" She snapped herself out of her daze.

"Our dancing."

"Oh, yeah. Definitely. It was so hot I need to go take a shower." She rolled her eyes and giggled some more as she abandoned the kitchen for their shared bathroom. If she was sweating a little, it was surely from nerves over what she was about to do, not because they'd affected her.

Sure.

She scrubbed herself then spent a while drying and curling her hair before applying what dashes of makeup she owned—a bit of mascara and some nude lip gloss. The whole time, she kept wondering what tonight might be like if she could spend it with someone she knew and trusted instead of gambling on a blind date set up by her well-meaning chemistry lab partner.

Andi bit her lip then harrumphed and fixed the damage, at least mentally reminding herself not to rub her eyes before she could wreck them too. She sighed then rested her forehead on the door, praying for some direction. Was she making a mistake? Or would it be an even bigger one to pursue the foolish ideas tempting her to feel out her roommates about her proposition?

Before she could make up her mind, a rap on the door rattled her brains.

"Ouch. Fuck." She stumbled back.

"Yo, Andi. Quit hogging. I drank three beers with dinner, and I gotta piss," Reed groaned. "I forgot what it's like to wait on someone trying to be girly."

Aaaaaaaaand... That sealed the deal.

They were too much like brothers to ever see her as a woman. Which was exactly how she'd wanted things while they lived together. She grinned as she opened the door. Reed squashed past her in the doorway, wedging them together when he froze. "Damn.

Uh, you look...great."

"The magic of wearing something other than sweats and one of your roommates' old shirts sans a bra." She shrugged.

"I kind of prefer the no-bra part." Simon waggled his

brows from where he scarfed another helping of now-cold pizza for second dinner.

When she turned to him with a smile, he paused mid-bite.

"What?" Andi finger-combed her hair as she stepped from the bathroom so Reed could relieve himself in peace. Not that the guys didn't invade her privacy often when she was in the shower, or vice versa. The trials of a single bathroom for four people had absolutely played a part in her collegiate years.

"I told you," Reed shouted through the door.

"They're right. You're hot." Cooper took her hand and spun her around. "I'm not sure we should let you go out like this, young lady."

"Whatever, Dad." She chuckled until he finished twirling her, though it hadn't entirely been a joke. With her parents both gone, these guys had stepped up and filled a huge, painful void as best they could. They were, and always would be, her family.

In the heels Andi had borrowed, she was closer to Cooper's height. Meeting his warm stare, she caught the spark of something serious there.

Could he actually be attracted to her?

She knew each of them appealed to her in various ways—Cooper's gentlemanliness and tact, Simon's playfulness and daring, Reed's sense of responsibility and control.

As if a sliver of possibility was the only prompt her subconscious required, she blurted the thoughts that had been haunting her for the past hour. Okay, longer than that. At least since she'd agreed to this outing. Probably since the day she co-signed their lease.

"Maybe you guys should come out too?" She prided

herself on the fact that she only stammered a little when she said, "Or I could stay home and we could have a private party instead."

Simon blinked at her, the pizza still lodged half-inside his mouth.

Cooper's fingers tightened around hers. His other hand landed at her waist to steady her. But he didn't say anything.

The door opening behind her broke the moment, forcing them apart.

Reed emerged as the toilet finished flushing in the background. It was as if her silly dreams circled the bowl then vanished down their clanky pipes when he grimaced. "What's that? Don't back out now. You've been looking forward to tonight all week. It's about time you cut loose. On your own. You've earned this."

"Oh. Okay." If they noticed the tremble in her faux smile, they didn't call her on it.

Andi decided to quit fucking around. Playing a game where she didn't know the rules was a sure way to lose. Reed was right. She had to learn to stand on her own, without leaning on them. Because in a matter of days, they wouldn't be part of her everyday existence anymore.

Graduation was a week away.

Her new life, the one where she'd be a lab tech in a prestigious pharmaceutical research firm—one that didn't include her roommates—was calling.

"Go ahead. Have fun," Simon said around a mouthful of pepperoni. "Besides, we've already—"

Cooper cleared his throat, but it was too late. She realized they must have dates. Of course they did.

"Hey, you'll be fine," he promised. He looked away before adding, "You don't need us."

Andi swallowed around the lump in her throat. She took a step forward and then another before grabbing her wristlet and keys out of the bowl at the end of the countertop.

If she was going to do this, she couldn't linger. Otherwise, she'd never convince herself to leave.

"Be safe!" Reed shouted as she closed the door softly behind her, determined not to let the stinging of her eyes turn into real tears and screw up her mascara.

To keep reading **4-Ever Theirs, click here.**

# WANT MORE MENAGE?

If you liked reading about this steamy non-traditional relationship, you should check out Nice & Naughty, another of Jayne's menage stories.

Can one man satisfy Alexa's appetites? Or will it take two?

After a disastrous lesson in heartache, Alexa Jones confines her adrenaline rushes to intense boardroom negotiations. Her legendary control cracks and she indulges in a high-octane encounter on the hood of her sports car. She never planned to see the enticing stranger again. When she finds herself across the boardroom table from him, there's suddenly more at stake than just her career.

Justin Winston got more than he bargained for on his summer drive, but he should have known nothing is ever that easy. He's met the woman of his dreams yet he doesn't know who she is. Luckily, he can always count on his practical brother for the things that matter, and this time is no exception. But, when a web of corporate espionage entangles them all, it's clear Justin isn't the only one who's fallen for their mysterious siren.

In Justin and Jason, Alexa finds something as unique and rare as the patent they will risk their lives to secure. The freedom to explore—and satisfy—the full range of her desires. From naughty to nice. Can Alexa accept the love of two men?

**Warning: This story contains light bondage, anal play and smoking hot brothers for double the fun and double the trouble.**

**An Excerpt From Nice & Naughty:**

"She's beautiful," he murmured reverently.

*The car. He's talking about your car.* She tried to convince herself, but the rationalization rang false. While he admired the convertible, something more arced between them. Attempting to shake off the unusual reaction inflaming her senses by focusing on her vehicle, Alexa stepped a little closer.

"I've done a lot of work on it."

"Can I touch her?" His implicit understanding of her dislike for people handling her vehicle made her confident he would treat it with the respect it deserved.

"Sure, go ahead." Plus, she got to watch the way his broad finger stroked the defined contour in the flawlessly waxed side panel, which inflamed her senses nearly as much as if he'd placed the caress on her skin instead.

Before she could stop to analyze what her subconscious offered, she asked, "Would you like to take a look under the hood?"

"Hell, yeah."

She had to laugh at the look on his face. "You look like a kid on Christmas."

"It's not every day I come across an opportunity like

this." The dark undercurrent of the statement and his piercing green stare made it clear he referred to more than a fancy sports car.

*Oh God. He feels it, too.*

Alexa should have been freaked out. Alone with a stranger, on a deserted stretch of highway, in the mountains far from the city, sounded like an unwise situation to put herself in. She should be nervous but a remarkable calm surrounded her instead. In fact, she just now realized she'd stopped on the side of the road without a second thought to safety. Today, she threw caution to the wind. The chemical reaction between them affected her like a drug.

As though he sensed her train of thought, the man backed away a few steps, displaying his non-threatening intent. He left the path clear for her to get in her car and drive away but her instincts shouted that she could trust him. She wanted to explore this attraction just a little bit further.

She leaned over the door and rested her fingertips on the hood release. The man's gaze tracked her movement yet he didn't encroach on her space. For a moment, the only sounds breaking the silence were the babble of the stream below, the gentle rustle of leaves from the tree branches overhead and a soft birdsong.

The air between them crackled with tension.

Then, the metallic click of the hood's latching mechanism disengaging relayed her decision to stay. A broad smile spread across his face, raising faint dimples that heightened his attractiveness. Alexa inclined her head in a "come here" gesture as she circled around to the front of the car.

He ambled to her side with a steady gait that made her

cognizant of his confidence she wouldn't run. Reaching for the edge of the hood simultaneously, their hands met. Sparks shot up her spine and she jerked. His arm wrapped around her waist in a protective hold. The solid strength kept her from losing her physical footing, but not her emotional balance. This close she could smell the unique combination of his leather gear and subtle, earthy cologne.

"Easy." His hand smoothed down her side and across the top of her ass as he went back to lifting the hood. The blatant touch imbued her with respect for his natural ability to handle a woman. However, she retained enough rationality to admire the gleaming chrome of the engine that she cleaned with painstaking diligence each weekend she could manage the time. Together they leaned forward, caught by the lure of a ridiculously overpowered motor.

"This is an aftermarket addition. Did you do this yourself?" His raised eyebrow conveyed his surprise.

"Yeah."

"I'm impressed. Are you a mechanic?"

"Nope, this is just a hobby." She smirked.

"Some hobby. I *am* a mechanic. This is a damn fine job."

Alexa basked in his appreciation for details. None of her friends understood her devotion to this machine. They couldn't comprehend why she spent the majority of her precious free time refining each tiny part until it was flawless. This man obviously did.

He ran his hand along the connections, searching with deft flicks of his fingertips for imperfections where none existed. His satisfied nod had her beaming.

"Jesus, woman. If someone told me I'd have the chance to play with a car like this today, I'd have said that nothing could distract me. But the way you're looking at me..."

His voice trailed off as she reached up to do a little exploring of her own. Her hand moved on autopilot, following her desire, cupping the side of his stubbled face.

*Is this guy for real?*

The wet heat of his lips on her palm rasped against her nerves, stronger than any dream. She whimpered as he turned his head to lick the center of her palm before catching the sensitive skin between her thumb and index finger in his teeth in a gentle nip. The move set her ablaze, destroying common sense.

"Kiss me," she demanded.

He didn't need to be told twice. With a low groan, he closed the narrow gap between them, sealing his mouth over hers. He dropped the hood in place and put his hand to better use, wrapping it around her hip, yanking her tight against the hard plane of his chest. His height made Alexa strain on tiptoes to return his kiss. Eager to help, he tucked his other hand around her thigh, just beneath the curve of her ass, and hoisted her up higher on his body.

They fit perfectly together.

Her hands tangled in his hair, loving the way the silky strands teased the sensitive crevices between her fingers. She kneaded his scalp, urging him to take her mouth deeper. His head angled over hers, intensifying the kiss as his tongue lashed playfully against the seam of her lips. She drew it inside her mouth and sucked. He tasted like peppermint.

She moaned with regret when he pulled away.

"I'm going to set you on the hood." He rumbled in her ear in between nibbles of her neck.

"No! Wait."

Though he looked disappointed, he stopped without hesitation.

The heat suffusing her face highlighted her discomfort with being so brazen. "I... I don't want to scratch the paint. Take my shorts off first."

Strained laughter burst from his chest. It transformed his features from rugged to unbearably handsome.

"Honey, you're my every fantasy."

To keep reading **Nice & Naughty, click here.**

# NAUGHTY NEWS

Want to win cool stuff? Get sneak peeks of upcoming books? How about being the first to know what's in the pipeline or where Jayne will be making appearances near you? If any of that stuff sounds good then sign up for Jayne's newsletter, the Naughty News. She never shares you information, pinky swear!

www.jaynerylon.com/newsletter

# WHAT WAS YOUR FAVORITE PART?

Did you enjoy this book? If so, please leave a review and tell your friends about it. Word of mouth and online reviews are immensely helpful and greatly appreciated.

# JAYNE'S SHOP

Check out Jayne's online shop for autographed print books, direct download ebooks, reading-themed apparel up to size 5XL, mugs, tote bags, notebooks, Mr. Rylon's wood (you'll have to see it for yourself!) and more.
www.jaynerylon.com/shop

# LISTEN UP!

The majority of Jayne's books are also available in audio format on Audible, Amazon and iTunes.

# GET IN TOUCH

*Jayne Loves To Hear From Readers*
www.jaynerylon.com
contact@jaynerylon.com

## ALSO BY JAYNE RYLON

4-EVER

*A New Adult Reverse Harem Series*

4-Ever Theirs

4-Ever Mine

EVER AFTER DUET

*Reverse Harem Featuring Characters From The 4-Ever Series*

Fourplay

Fourkeeps

POWERTOOLS

*Five Guys Who Get It On With Each Other & One Girl. Enough Said?*

Kate's Crew

Morgan's Surprise

Kayla's Gift

Devon's Pair

Nailed to the Wall

Hammer it Home

More the Merrier *NEW*

HOT RODS

*Powertools Spin Off. Keep up with the Crew plus...*

*Seven Guys & One Girl. Enough Said?*

King Cobra

Mustang Sally

Super Nova

Rebel on the Run

Swinger Style

Barracuda's Heart

Touch of Amber

Long Time Coming

## HOT RIDES

*Powertools and Hot Rods Spin Off.*

*Menage and Motorcycles*

Wild Ride - Coming Soon!

Slow Ride - Coming Soon!

Rough Ride - Coming Soon!

Ride - Coming Soon!

Ride - Coming Soon!

## MEN IN BLUE

*Hot Cops Save Women In Danger*

Night is Darkest

Razor's Edge

Mistress's Master

Spread Your Wings

Wounded Hearts

Bound For You

## DIVEMASTERS

*Sexy SCUBA Instructors By Day, Doms On A Mega-Yacht By Night*

Going Down

Going Deep

Going Hard


STANDALONE

*Menage*

*Middleman*

Nice & Naughty

*Contemporary*

Where There's Smoke

Report For Booty


COMPASS BROTHERS

*Modern Western Family Drama Plus Lots Of Steamy Sex*

Northern Exposure

Southern Comfort

Eastern Ambitions

Western Ties


COMPASS GIRLS

*Daughters Of The Compass Brothers Drive Their Dads Crazy And Fall In Love*

Winter's Thaw

Hope Springs

Summer Fling

Falling Softly


COMPASS BOYS

*Sons Of The Compass Brothers Fall In Love*

Heaven on Earth

Into the Fire

Still Waters

Light as Air


PLAY DOCTOR

*Naughty Sexual Psychology Experiments Anyone?*

Dream Machine

Healing Touch


RED LIGHT

*A Hooker Who Loves Her Job*

Complete Red Light Series Boxset

FREE - Through My Window - FREE

Star

Can't Buy Love

Free For All


PICK YOUR PLEASURES

*Choose Your Own Adventure Romances!*

Pick Your Pleasure

Pick Your Pleasure 2


RACING FOR LOVE

*MMF Menages With Race-Car Driver Heroes*

Complete Series Boxset

Driven

Shifting Gears

PARANORMALS

*Vampires, Witches, And A Man Trapped In A Painting*

Paranormal Double Pack Boxset

Picture Perfect

Reborn


PENTHOUSE PLEASURES

*Naughty Manhattanite Neighbors Find Kinky Love*

Taboo

Kinky

Sinner

35765348R00109

Made in the USA
Lexington, KY
07 April 2019